THE COST OF LOVE

AN EROTIC TALE OF SEDUCTION, DECEPTION, AND UNDYING DEVOTION

TINA TENNYSON

Inspired Forever Books
Dallas, Texas

The Cost of Love: An Erotic Tale of Seduction, Deception, and Undying Devotion

© 2021 Tina Tennyson

Inspired Forever Books™
"Words with Lasting Impact"
Dallas, Texas
(888) 403-2727
https://inspiredforeverbooks.com

Library of Congress Control Number: 2020903351

Paperback ISBN 13: 978-1-948903-31-8

Printed in the United States of America

TABLE OF CONTENTS

CHAPTER 1

Bianca awoke in a blissful mood to the alarm buzzing from her cellphone. She'd always been a morning person, and on this particular day, the sun was casting gold beams through the vertical blinds covering the windows in her master bedroom.

She could hear Kevin as he brushed his teeth, getting ready to head out the door for work. Kevin was an attorney at Windsor and Boone Law Firm. He had been there for two years and was climbing the ladder quickly.

Bianca sat up in their queen-sized bed and thought about the love of her life. They had been together since college, having met in law school during her second year and his third.

He had asked her out several times before she reluctantly said yes—she had wanted to focus solely on her studies, not on a man. But Kevin was special. They had hit it off immediately and had been together ever since. Bianca had started baking pastries for their study group, and everything she baked was a hit. Their study group went from three people to fifteen in a matter of weeks. Bianca had started baking more than she was studying, so when test time came, she failed. To heal her

1

emotional wounds, Bianca made the best double chocolate cake that she had ever baked, and she had an epiphany. She invested the remainder of the money she had saved for law school into opening a small bakery on the north side of Dallas.

Six months after her bakery's grand opening, she and Kevin were married—the perfect icing on the cake, and she felt abundantly blessed to have found passion in both her marriage and her career.

They had moved into this duplex four years ago, and while money was fairly good, Bianca's shopping habits and Kevin's increasingly regular cravings for the euphoric effects of shrooms ate up a chunk of their budget. They paid all their bills, but any money left over seemed to disappear quickly. And from Bianca's perspective, Kevin's usage had been on the uptick for the past few weeks. Or was that just her overactive imagination?

Snapping back to the present, Bianca jumped out of bed and headed to the bathroom, wearing an oversized pink t-shirt with nothing underneath. She kissed Kevin's cheek.

"Good morning, love," she purred. "Let me jump in the shower, and I'll be ready in just a minute."

Kevin, still wearing just a towel and brushing his teeth, smiled in response.

She passed him and turned on the shower, tossing her pink shirt to the floor. The hot water ignited her senses, steaming the bathroom and building upon the warmth already growing inside her.

Minutes later, Bianca turned off the water and grabbed her robe. Kevin had already left the bathroom and was standing in the bedroom wearing black slacks. He was putting one arm in his shirt when Bianca stepped into the room.

Kevin looked at her passionately.

Bianca dropped her robe to reveal skin that was still glistening with moisture and walked toward him. The fresh scent of vanilla emanated from her skin.

Kevin stopped fixing his shirt, and Bianca unbuckled his pants.

They began to kiss. Kevin nibbled on her lips with mild aggression; she moaned in pleasure. Breaking their lips, she pushed him backward onto the bed.

Kevin fell back with ease, revealing his full erection. Bianca climbed on top of his legs and released his now throbbing manhood from his pants. She took him into her mouth halfway, and Kevin inhaled. She began to move her head up and down slowly for about a minute, then climbed on top of him and began to grind slowly.

Kevin grabbed her hips, pushing himself deeper inside of her, and she began to moan loudly. Kevin guided her hips and increased their speed, feeling her climax building. His breathing became rough and ragged.

As she rode, Bianca's eyes closed in ecstasy.

A loud, forceful knock on their front door threatened the mood. Bianca's face frowned, but her eyes stayed closed. She ignored the sound, trying to maintain her rhythm.

The knock came again, harder and more insistent this time, as though the person doing the pounding would be entering their duplex soon whether they opened the door or not.

Bianca's eyes opened, but instead of seeing Kevin beneath her, she found herself sitting on the recliner in her dark living room.

The knock came again, louder and harder.

Disoriented, Bianca searched in the darkness for the direction of the sound. Her eyes landed on the back door that led from her kitchen to a patio. Frozen by fear and confusion, Bianca couldn't move.

The knock came again.

She rose to her feet and walked slowly toward the back door, not sure if she was ready to open it. She stared at the black silhouette that was visible through the blinds covering the glass door.

"I know you're in there," the male voice cracked.

Bianca reluctantly stepped forward, turned the two locks on the door, and opened it to reveal Kevin, draped in filthy clothes and looking as though he hadn't bathed in weeks. His hair was messy and overgrown, and his mustache and beard were beginning to take over his entire face.

Bianca stood in the doorway, the screen door still a barrier between them.

Kevin smiled.

Even in his unkempt condition, Bianca's heart melted when the dimple on his cheek that she loved so much made its appearance.

"I knew you would answer." There was hope in his voice.

She looked him up and down, noticing the hole in his shoe now that she was close enough to get a full image of him, and unlocked the screen door.

He pulled the handle immediately, and she moved aside to allow him into the duplex that they had once shared.

She walked to the fridge and pulled out a plate covered in plastic wrap and placed it in the microwave. Kevin had already begun to take his clothes off at the door, and by the time Bianca had set the cook timer, he was down to his boxers.

Without the ill-fitting, soiled clothes of a homeless person, Kevin became Kevin again, and Bianca admired that his body was still immaculate. She grabbed the filthy clothes that littered her white tile floor and opened the cabinet under the sink to grab a trash bag, noting a foul odor that she assumed had been germinating in the fabric for weeks.

Kevin was already on his way to the master bathroom to take a shower.

Bianca double-bagged his clothes and remembered that he had walked out of the kitchen still wearing those disgusting boxers. She dropped the bag on the floor and headed to her bathroom to collect them. As she approached her bedroom door, she could hear Kevin singing in the shower. Her heart began to pound. That was one of the things she missed the most—the sound of his voice.

It felt like almost overnight he had gone from shrooms to more hardcore drugs. Even with cocaine in his system, Kevin had been able to function at home and at work, but once he was introduced to heroin, darkness and destruction followed. Bianca had been completely blindsided when Kevin began to steal from her.

First, it was money from her purse. Then electronics started to disappear. After he had gone missing for three days and appeared at home late one evening as though nothing had happened, Bianca knew she had a serious problem on her hands.

She had repeatedly asked and eventually begged him to go into a rehabilitation program. For months he had refused, insisting that he was fine and had everything under control.

His surrender came one night after he had been beaten to a pulp. He had been given credit on some product and had never made good on the debt. Like this night, he had pounded on her door, begging for entry. She had kicked him out just two months earlier, after his repeated refusals to enter rehab. Plus, there wasn't any amount of love that could make her forget that he would steal whatever he wanted when he was ready to get high again. She'd had enough.

Standing at her door, covered in his own blood, his left eye swollen shut, he had finally agreed to rehab.

Rehab was a short-lived dream, as Kevin didn't last five days before demanding to be released. With no court order stating that he had to remain in treatment, Kevin was back out on the streets. He broke into Bianca's duplex and stole the flat-screen TV and Blu-ray player that were in the living room.

Bianca had stopped by her sister's house after work that night to discuss the stresses of owning her own bakery and dealing with Kevin. Her sister was a great listener who offered great wine, and after several glasses, Bianca had opted to spend the night.

She was taken aback when she returned home the next morning to find her front door ajar. She flipped on the light inside the door and panicked. Inside, she found broken glass where someone had also broken a window, and she noticed right away the missing items in the living room.

She flashed back from the uncomfortable memory, still sickened by how far and how fast he had fallen. She collected his boxers and listened to the beautiful music coming from the man who was still legally her husband. The man who had made her truly happy once.

She chose not to interrupt him, though she was sure he had heard her enter the bathroom, and walked back to the kitchen.

She gathered up the trash bags and headed to the trash can on her patio. She breathed in the warmth of the nighttime summer air, steeling herself for whatever would lie ahead, and went back inside.

When she reached her bedroom, Kevin was standing in the bathroom doorway, wearing nothing but a towel.

Bianca remembered her dream and felt a moment of déjà vu.

This was the fourth time he had come to her door begging for entry in the last four months. They had been living apart for six.

By this time, she had their routine down. He came, showered, and ate. Sometimes he left immediately, but the last time he had asked to sleep on the couch. Knowing that he would be safe at least for a night, Bianca had relented. She looked at him now and wondered if tonight would be another night that he stayed. She was feeling compassionate enough to allow him to sleep in their bed.

"What are you looking at?" His question brought her from her thoughts.

"Nothing," she said as she bit her bottom lip, watching the beads of water that glistened on his chest.

She walked to a large chest of drawers where she kept clean clothes for him and selected undergarments, a shirt, and a pair of pants. As she moved closer to the bedroom door, he stepped into the room, inching closer to her before she could exit. Their arms brushed lightly as she paused for a second to place the clothes on a chair by her bedroom door.

"Here are some clean clothes. Get dressed, and I'll meet you in the kitchen." She took another step forward, and he grabbed her arm, rubbing his hand down it.

"Thanks for the shower."

She quivered at his touch but didn't speak. She froze for a few seconds, remembering how it felt to simply be in his embrace. She shook her head silently while reminding herself that she couldn't relive the past. That ship had sailed on a wave of lies and deceit.

"I'll meet you in the kitchen," she repeated, and continued down the hallway.

Bianca went straight to the microwave to check that the leftover chicken breast, macaroni and cheese, and broccoli was warm enough to eat. Tasting the food she had prepared a few days before, she smiled, delighted with its warmth. As she moved the plate from the microwave to the bar top, Kevin emerged from her bedroom, wearing a dark gray V-neck t-shirt and black jeans. Now that he had cleaned up, he was starting to look more like himself, she thought.

He walked over to the bar. "All of this for me?"

Bianca nodded her head with a smile.

Kevin took the plate from the bar and walked toward the small round wooden table in the dining room.

As he ate, Bianca came around the bar and sat across from him in silence. She watched as he ravaged the plate of food before him.

When he got down to the last bite, he lifted his head. Reaching his other arm from underneath the table, he touched her hand.

"I always did love your home-cooked meals." Kevin caressed her fingers.

Bianca pulled her hand back and stood from the table.

"Should I get a blanket and pillow for the couch?" Her voice was unsteady when she spoke.

Kevin stood at that moment and wiped his hands together to show that he was finished.

She turned back and looked at him as he approached her. As he came up behind her, his hand touched her back.

"No, not tonight, love. I have some things I need to take care of."

He moved past her and went back to the kitchen door that he had entered just an hour before.

She followed him to the door, surprised at the amount of sadness in her heart.

He paused once he reached the door, allowing her to catch up, and turned around to face her.

Bianca was caught off guard when he wrapped her in an embrace.

"Thank you."

She felt Kevin's lips brush the top of her forehead, and he released her.

She stepped back and allowed him to exit, watching him from the doorway as he maneuvered his way out of her enclosed back yard the same way he had entered.

She shut the door and turned every lock, then just stood there for a moment in a daze, wondering if he would return.

CHAPTER 2

Sleep escaped her as she tossed and turned throughout the remaining hours before daylight. She was actually relieved when the alarm went off. Staring at the white ceiling, she pulled the comforter back and listened to the alarm, not wanting to silence it. She thought about how much she loved Kevin and how things had spiraled out of control. She blamed herself for not recognizing the signs of his addiction. He had always reassured her, telling her that it was just for fun—just a way for him to relax.

I don't say anything to you when you're on your fourth glass of wine, she remembered him mocking her. She thought about the first time he had left on a Friday night and hadn't come home until Monday afternoon. Then she thought about last night and how shabby he had looked. Kevin was still an attractive man, but his drug usage was beginning to show in his face. She had noticed for the first time the wrinkles that were starting to etch his once smooth complexion. Thirty-two is too young for wrinkles. Bianca sighed.

The alarm continued to interrupt her thoughts, and Bianca sat up. She had to open the shop this morning. She had been meaning to make a spare key for Vivian, her assistant, who

11

was a pretty, brown-skinned woman with a thick bottom and large breasts. Even though she usually tried to cover them, they spilled out of almost every V-neck shirt or dress she wore to the bakery. Her uniform apron helped provide some coverage. Bianca decided that she would make the extra key today so that some days she could sleep in just a little longer.

Having made up her mind, she walked to the bathroom, pulled the shower curtain back, turned on the water, and adjusted it to the hot temperature she enjoyed.

As she undressed, she caught a glimpse of herself in the mirror. She turned to face the mirror and examined her body. For a baker, she was medium-sized in figure. Her breasts were large, and her hips and ass were proportionately curvy. Her stomach wasn't completely flat; she had a small pudge that only a strict workout schedule had ever resolved. And lately she just hadn't had the time.

I need to go back to working out three days a week. Cupcakes are finally starting to get to me, she thought. And with that, she entered the hot, steamy shower.

After about ten minutes, she exited the shower and grabbed her towel from behind the bathroom door. She went immediately to her bedroom closet. She grabbed black casual slacks and a purple silk blouse. She went over to her chest of drawers and selected black cotton boy shorts and a black cotton bra.

Placing the items on her unmade bed, she went back to her dresser and picked up her favorite lotion, At the Beach, by Bath & Body Works.

After she applied the lotion and dressed, she walked out of her bedroom and headed to the kitchen. She turned on her black Keurig and grabbed her favorite pink mug from the dish rack. Her coffee of choice this morning was Michigan Cherry.

She placed the pod in the maker and her cup underneath, selected the size cup she wanted, and walked away.

Standing at her small kitchen island, she allowed the aroma of coffee to fill the area. She breathed it in heavily, anticipating the taste that would be on her tongue soon. She looked over at the dining room table and noticed her purse looked open. Forgetting completely the blissful feeling she had felt only seconds before, her heart sank to the floor.

She walked over to her large crossbody bag and looked inside. The cash she had placed neatly in there yesterday had been ruffled. Bianca took the money out and counted it. Then she counted it again. After the fourth time, every muscle in her body felt tense as her anger built. One hundred dollars was missing.

"Shit," she yelled out loud.

Today was her day to pay the landlord for the small building she rented to run her bakery, and now she was one hundred dollars short of the twelve hundred she paid each month. It was clear where the money had gone. Bianca's blood began to boil.

"Kevin, you fucking thief!" The words spewed from her lips like venom.

As much as she loved him, shit like this always made her second-guess herself for unlocking that door for him. And this might just be the last time, she thought to herself.

She stuffed the money back into her purse in frustration and anger.

What the hell was she going to do about the missing money? she wondered, throwing her purse down on the glass table. She began to pace. She thought about her landlord. Frank Reynolds was a brown-skinned man in his fifties who had a belly that hung over top of his pants, which were always secured by a belt that looked way too tight. Mr. Reynolds was a stern landlord who gave no leeway when the rent for the place was due. He casually walked into her bakery the first Tuesday of every month, ready to collect the rent and the strawberry strudels that she made especially for him. Her pastries are what had convinced him to agree to the lease after reviewing her credit and seeing the $80,000 debt that Bianca had accumulated in her years of unfinished education. Getting a business loan had been impossible for her with all the odds stacked against her.

She had walked by the small gray building with the For Lease sign in the window for several days before finally mustering up her courage and calling the number.

Mr. Reynolds had originally denied her application for the property and had sent her a letter in the mail that advised her of his denial. Bianca had been upset, and Kevin had been no help. His solution had been for her to simply forget about the bakery and re-enroll in law school.

That night in her frustration, Bianca had made two chocolate cakes, vanilla cream cheese cupcakes, and strawberry strudels.

Exhaustion had finally hit around five in the morning, and she retired to bed with Kevin, only for him to get out of bed a few hours later to go to Windsor and Boone. She had been too tired to get up as he moved around the duplex, collecting his things and finally exiting. She had waited until she heard the door lock and closed her eyes, welcoming the feeling of solitude.

Bianca had rolled out of bed a few hours later with a gem of an idea. She quickly dressed in a flowy yellow dress with a yellow belt that fit perfectly around her waist and accentuated her curves. She armed herself with a pink box that contained cupcakes and strudels, and she left their duplex on a mission. She had walked the two and a half blocks it took to get to the building and had made it there in perfect time, as there were two men surveying the area, locked in conversation.

She had walked inside the building, commanding their attention with her grand entrance, her yellow dress and pink bakery box both welcome pops of color in an otherwise drab, empty building.

She recalled her interaction with Frank Reynolds with perfect clarity.

"Excuse the intrusion gentlemen. I have a delivery for . . . ," she said, pretending to look for a receipt. "A Mr. Reynolds." She looked up at the men.

Mr. Reynolds stepped forward, his eyes staring at the pink box with curiosity.

"I'm Mr. Reynolds." He began to walk toward Bianca, and his eyes widened with hunger as he caught the first whiff of fresh-baked pastries.

Bianca smiled. From the size of his belly and the look in his eyes, she knew that she had him hooked on her line. She peered over his shoulder at the man with whom he'd been speaking and noticed that his curiosity had been piqued as well. Her smile widened.

As soon as Mr. Reynolds got close enough to her, she offered him the box.

He snapped open the top and looked down at the cupcakes and strawberry strudels. Without hesitation, he reached his hand inside and took out a strawberry strudel. He ate it quickly, then another one, then another. He licked his fingers, now ready to speak.

"Where did you say these were from?" His words were slightly muffled as he chewed the last of the pastry in his mouth.

"I didn't," she smiled. "My name is Bianca Mansfield, and I'd like you to reconsider my application to lease this space for my bakery. What do you say?" She extended her hand.

Frank Reynolds looked down at the box of pastries, then back at the man who was still standing behind him. Then his eyes trailed to Bianca's eyes, then to her extended hand. For a brief moment, he stood there with a look of confusion. Then he looked at the box of pastries again, and his mouth watered.

"As long as I get a box of strudels every month with your rent, the place is yours." He picked up a cupcake and took a large bite.

"Shit! You have got to be fucking kidding me! We were just about to make the deal, Frank. Are pastries worth more than my business proposal?" the other man protested as he walked forward to join them.

Finishing the cupcake, Mr. Reynolds said, "Call me Mr. Reynolds, and vacate this woman's property." He looked at Bianca, who had finally put her hand down.

"This is bullshit!" the man yelled as he stormed out of the building.

Bianca stood in front of Mr. Reynolds with a feeling of triumph, but it was short-lived.

Mr. Reynolds' polite tone changed to more of a vicious one, like he was angry about something she had done to him personally.

"So, do we have a deal, what was it? Ms. Mansfield?"

Bianca didn't know whether to stand up to the challenge or

run from the building in fear. Suddenly, it seemed as though he was towering over her.

"Strudels would be no prob-," she didn't get to finish before Mr. Reynolds spoke again.

"Good. Because I expect the rent to be on time every month. The first Tuesday of every month. If you're late once, you're out! You're short with the money, you're out! If you approach me with personal problems, you're out! I don't give a damn about your life or your problems! Have the rent when your rent's due or you're out! Am I making myself clear?" He took a step forward, almost knocking her over, as she felt his breath on her face.

"Sure, no problem, Mr. Reynolds. I will not disappoint you," she said firmly.

Mr. Reynolds smiled and stepped back in front of the box of pastries that now sat to the left of him on a counter.

"Great. I will have to bring back some paperwork with your name on it. Can you come back tomorrow at eleven in the morning?"

Bianca's smile reappeared.

"Yes, sir, I can!" She put her hand out again for Mr. Reynolds to take, and this time he grabbed her hand and squeezed it tightly.

"Don't be late," he commanded, releasing her hand.

"I won't," she confirmed. And with that, she exited the building.

She practically skipped the entire way home. Her dream was about to take shape. She laughed at her forwardness and felt weird about Mr. Reynolds' sudden change in mood. But she could not help but be happy that she had gotten the place she wanted. That day, Pastries From Paradise was born.

Bianca came back to the present moment and began pacing the floor again. She knew there was no way in hell she could be late with the rent, and there was no such thing as working out a deal with Mr. Reynolds. She stopped in her tracks as she remembered something.

Running to the bedroom, she went to her closet and shoved aside the shoe boxes that littered the floor, grabbing one in the very back. Bianca sat on the floor and flipped open the box. Inside were tan suede wedges. Bianca put her hand inside one of the shoes and pulled out a wad of cash that appeared to be mostly one-dollar bills. Bianca counted out fifty-three dollars.

She reached her hand into the other shoe and pulled out another wad of one-dollar bills. This time she counted out thirty-eight.

Shit, she thought as she piled the money in one hand. She was still nine dollars short.

She threw the money onto her bed and went straight for her dirty clothes basket. She pulled out every pair of jeans she could find, searching through the pockets for any leftover change.

With clothes scattered across her bedroom floor, Bianca stood victorious. She had found a total of eighteen dollars. She threw that money onto the bed with the rest of the cash, then picked up the scattered clothes and placed them back in the basket.

She counted out one hundred dollars and headed toward the dining room. She flipped open her purse and collected the money inside. She combined the stacks of money and counted it.

She counted it a second time and then a third. Twelve hundred dollars exactly. She praised the high heaven that she had a habit of squirreling away money in secret places so that when she was ready for a night out, for a day at the spa, or at least a massage once a month, she could treat herself.

The bakery was doing well with her usual customers and the occasional catering gig or large order. She was clearing just enough to take care of all the bills at home and at the bakery. She wasn't complaining. Just enough would have to do since her split with Kevin. When they were together, he had taken care of most of the bills, leaving Bianca with a sense of security. Whether the bakery did well or not, Bianca had known that Kevin's income would provide them with a comfortable life.

Of course, all that had changed since the drugs had taken such a strong hold on him. Bianca didn't want to think about it. She forced herself to come back to the present.

Still holding the money, she folded it and put it safely inside her bag, snapping it shut, and pulling the strap over her head. Carrying so much cash always made her anxious, but it was another concession she had to make for Mr. Reynolds thanks to her credit history.

She walked to the front door and took one last look around, making sure she had turned off the lights before leaving the duplex.

She walked to the bakery, not in a rush but not at a slow pace either. As she walked, she took in the scenery of the other homes and the cars going by until she made it to the main street.

A line of three or four people had already formed outside the bakery. They represented some of her regulars who started their days with a morning coffee and a pastry. Her desperate search to replace the missing money had caused her to be a bit later than usual. She really needed to get that key made for Vivian, she thought. She made sure she was smiling as she approached.

"Good morning, Bianca," Vivian greeted her with a smile.

"Good morning, everyone!" Bianca said as she moved through the people and made it to the glass front door. She turned the lock and flipped on the open sign.

As soon as she entered, she went behind the corner and pressed the start button on her coffee maker.

Vivian joined her behind the counter and moved past her to turn on the ovens and get the pastries and donuts that Bianca had prepared the day before.

The bakery began to smell like coffee and pastries. Bianca inhaled deeply and then spoke loud enough for everyone in the shop to hear.

"It will be just a few minutes before everything is ready. I appreciate everyone's patience," she said with a smile.

Her loyal customers returned her smile and nodded their agreement.

Within ten minutes, the first tray of pastries had been baked to perfection. Donuts, bear claws, cheese and strawberry danishes, and donut holes beckoned to be smelled and tasted.

Vivian slid another tray into the giant oven, and one of their regular customers, Ben, approached the counter.

"Good morning, Ben." Bianca gave him a personal greeting.

"Good morning, Ms. B. I would like a cup of premium roast coffee and two bear claws," he smiled back.

"Two bear claws! So much for that diet you were talking about starting last week!" she joked.

His mouth began to water as Vivian selected two bear claws from the tray.

"What diet?" he asked playfully, his voice low as he eyed the bear claws.

Bianca burst into laughter.

"Your pastries are too good to even consider a diet! I'm sure I was just blowing smoke."

She laughed again. "Is this for here or to go?"

"To go. I have an important meeting today."

Bianca looked up at the clock on the wall and noticed that it was already eight-thirty.

Ben paid for his order, and Bianca handed him his coffee and white paper bag with his two freshly made bear claws.

"Thank you, Ms. B. Your pastries change lives!" This time it was Ben's turn to burst into laughter.

Bianca laughed as Ben walked toward the door. "Have a great day, Ben!"

"I plan on it!" Ben said, exiting the pastry shop.

Bianca happily greeted the next customer as Vivian repeated the ritual of removing a finished tray and inserting another one.

Turning around to make a mocha latte, Bianca didn't see Mr. Reynolds come in.

He had taken a seat near the door, and when Bianca turned to hand the mocha latte to the customer, he rose from the chair.

People continued to trickle into the bakery.

"Vivian, I need you to take over the register for me."

Vivian turned around from wiping down the counters and spotted Mr. Reynolds. She frowned briefly and replaced Bianca at the register.

Bianca stepped away and greeted Mr. Reynolds with a forced smile and a "good morning" at the opposite end of the counter.

"I'm here to collect your rent," Mr. Reynolds said sternly. He certainly wasn't one for small talk.

Grabbing her crossbody from under her side of the counter, Bianca walked toward a nearby table and sat. Mr. Reynolds followed closely behind her, almost on her heels.

She pulled out an envelope filled with cash and handed it to Mr. Reynolds, whose scowl turned into an approving smirk.

"Thank you, but I think you're forgetting something."

Knowing exactly what he was referring to, Bianca looked back at the main counter and saw Vivian still hard at work, taking and preparing orders.

"No, Mr. Reynolds. I don't think so."

She got up from the table and went behind the counter. She grabbed a medium-sized pink pastry box and stuffed six strawberry strudels inside.

With the box in her hand, ready to be rid of her landlord, she spoke again.

"This should cover it." She reached out the box to him.

Mr. Reynolds stood and grabbed the box from her hand and began to walk toward the front door.

"Have a great day, Mr. Reynolds!" Bianca called out as earnestly as she could.

He grumbled something under his breath and exited the building.

Two more people came in behind him.

Bianca looked around the room. It was the morning rush, and Pastries From Paradise was beginning to fill up. There were only a few open seats.

She was glad to be rid of her landlord's judgmental eyes and disapproving stares. Each month, he waited for her to give an excuse why she was unable to pay her rent, and each month, she had paid him on the day that he arrived and handed him a box of strawberry strudels.

Bianca had always held up her end of the bargain, but Mr. Reynolds was clearly not the type of man to let his guard down for any reason. To him, a show of compassion was surely a sign of weakness, and he never let her forget that he had done her a favor by ignoring her credit history and renting the space to her. To him, she was indebted to him for as long as he saw fit. Bianca frowned at that thought, but she loved her small bakery and prided herself on not being late once.

Feeling triumphant over her minor setback with the stolen money this morning, she inhaled deeply. Letting out the breath, her smile reappeared, and she went behind the counter to resume her duties. At least this place was one less thing she had to worry about.

The rest of the day went by without a snag in detail, each person delighted as they exited her little slice of heaven. Bianca was jovial as she imagined the register overflowing with money while she swept the shop floor, preparing to close for the evening.

Bianca looked up at the clock. It was nearly six. Pastries From Paradise would be closing in five minutes.

She looked around the room. All the customers had left, and there didn't appear to be any stray belongings left behind that she should put behind the counter for safe keeping. It was amazing how many times a phone charger was forgotten or a coat was left behind on one of the chairs.

Only she and Vivian remained, and she smiled with satisfaction. At last the day was complete.

She walked behind the counter to put away the broom as Vivian loaded the dishwasher with eight pastry trays and all the utensils, plates, and coffee mugs.

Bianca thought about her rough night's sleep and the even rougher morning that she had awoken to. How could Kevin steal from her again? If he came knocking on her door again, could she honestly turn him away? Her attitude toward him had softened after a successful day at the bakery, and she considered the notion that Kevin's habit of stealing was something she might have to get used to. The idea was agonizing.

Vivian had just closed the large dishwasher and started the wash cycle when Bianca approached and leaned on the other side of the counter, looking in her direction deep in thought but not actually looking at her. Vivian had seen that look before. She leaned against the dishwasher and folded her arms.

"Have you heard from Kevin?"

This question brought Bianca back to the present as her eyes met Vivian's.

"He came by last night but didn't stay," Bianca said, almost at a whisper.

Vivian immediately got excited and approached the counter, smiling from ear to ear.

"I told you he would be back, Bianca! So, you two ready to make up yet?" Vivian propped her hand under her chin and smiled dreamily. "Does this mean he is finally serious about his recovery? You two have been my favorite couple for as long as I have known you."

Bianca put up her hand, signaling for Vivian not to say any more.

"He isn't going to rehab. He is probably somewhere getting high at this very moment with the hundred dollars that he stole from my purse last night." Bianca closed her eyes, attempting to stop the tears that were beginning to fall.

Watching her boss and best friend break down in tears, Vivian walked around the counter and embraced Bianca tightly as she cried.

"I'm so sorry. Things will get better." Vivian's voice was soothing.

Bianca didn't speak. She just continued to cry on the shoulder of her true confidant.

CHAPTER 3

Kevin awoke with a mind still foggy from the drugs. The filthy mattress beneath him had no doubt come from a dumpster. He didn't move much as he stared up at a ceiling that was dappled with water spots and pock-marked by peeling paint.

In his state of confusion, Kevin had no idea where the hell he was and didn't care. All he knew was that his high had gone down, and it was time to find a way to get his hands on more cash.

He thought about the money that he had slipped into his pocket from Bianca's purse and felt absolutely no emotion about his theft.

He had blown through that hundred dollars in only a few hours, meeting up with his usual dealer before heading to a familiar abandoned house, where other heroin addicts had made a safe haven for using. The abandoned house was just six blocks away from where he used to live with Bianca.

Kevin sat up and saw two other people lying on the hard-wood floor, which was badly stained with urine, rainwater from the ceiling, and the overall filth that had accumulated in this abandoned space. The stench of mildew mixed with urine filled the air. The room appeared to be the master bedroom of the house. Someone had placed newspapers over all the windows, darkening the room to some degree and making it difficult to predict the time of day.

A body on the floor began to stir, and Kevin's eyes followed as a young African-American woman, still wobbly, rose to her feet. She sashayed over to where Kevin still sat on the end of the bed. She wore a dirty yellow dress covered in multiple stains from only God knows what. The dress reached about midway down her thighs. The wig she wore was slightly turned to the side, and the makeup that was smeared across her face looked as though it had been there for weeks.

If the young woman had not been on heroin, she might have been beautiful. But the drugs had taken a toll, leaving her with horribly dry skin in some places, and black marks and acne in other places.

She began to dance to a song no one could hear except for her, swaying back and forth.

"You like this, Daddy? Just another hit and I'm all yours."

Kevin looked at the woman with disgust and pity in his eyes.

She stepped forward, attempting to climb on his lap.

Standing up quickly, Kevin pushed her to the floor.

She yelled in exaggerated agony, waking up the other person in the room, who was male.

The man jumped up in full-on attack mode.

"What the fuck are you doing with my woman?" The man tried to sound threatening, but his body looked feeble.

Kevin could tell that he was envious that Kevin looked so clean in such a filthy place.

The man stood next to the woman on the floor, who stared glassy-eyed as though the devil had entered the room.

"I said, what the fuck are you doing with my woman?" he roared.

Not taking another second to think about it, Kevin hit the man with a right hook, then a left, punching him in the nose before he fell back. The young woman shrieked in horror as her man hit the floor out cold.

The woman scrambled on the floor to where the man's body was lying.

"Tony, Tony? You OK, baby? Wake up!" she shrieked. "Wake up! Baby, get up!"

She attempted to shake him awake. When he didn't move, she jumped to her feet and charged toward Kevin.

"You fucking killed him!" she screamed. "You fucking bastard!"

Before she was able to lay a hand on him, Kevin's reflexes kicked in, and he punched the young woman in the face, knocking her out cold. She landed just a few inches from her boyfriend.

Standing in the quietness of the room once more, Kevin finally spoke.

"You see what the fuck you made me do?" His words were venomous as he looked down at the unconscious couple. He spit in the couple's direction and exited the room.

The house was one level, so Kevin could see the front door as he stood in the hallway, waiting to see if any of the other junkies wanted a piece of him today.

He walked down the hall, being careful not to step on any of the other bodies. No one else stirred or even acknowledged his presence. As he walked past the living room to the front door, he noticed two more dirty mattresses with a person on each and three more people scattered around the room, lying on the hardwood floor. He had to get the hell out of there.

He made his way to the front door and opened it, spilling sunlight into the dark space. He stepped into the bright sun, a man on a mission to obtain money.

He knew it was only a matter of time before Bianca noticed her missing cash, so going to her place to scout for easy pickings was not an option.

Kevin thought about the people he had just left in the abandoned house. Comparing himself to them, he thought, I am not as bad as those people. I have complete control of this situation. I can stop whenever I am ready.

He looked down at himself. His clothes were still clean for the most part. As he walked down the residential street, he passed someone.

"Hey, my brother," Kevin spoke with confidence. "Can you tell me what day it is?"

The man stopped and looked momentarily confused by the question.

"It's Tuesday, man. June 25." And with that, the man continued his stride.

Kevin realized that he had been in that abandoned house for five days.

"I have everything under control," he said out loud, attempting to reassure himself of his own strength and power.

Yes, he loved heroin. The high was like nothing he had ever felt before, and it was well worth turning a blind eye to his losses. He had lost his job and been disbarred; he'd failed miserably at rehab and lost his wife. But he could not fight the urge for his next hit—not that he had any intention of quitting. The high made him feel euphoric and invincible, and he was not willing to give that up under any circumstances.

And why should he have to? As for everything he had done up until that point, when he was good and ready he could make amends. He knew that Bianca loved him no matter what, and even though he had stolen from her, there was close to nothing that she would not do for him. He knew that all she wanted was for him to recover.

But Kevin wasn't quite ready for recovery. He thought about the painful, tortured hell his body would have to endure if he ever made such a commitment.

"Hell no," he said out loud again to no one as he continued to walk. Luckily, he was alone now on the sidewalk. There was no one to pay attention to his outburst.

Over the past few months, Kevin had gotten pretty slick at pick-pocketing people in large crowds. Depending on the time of day, the nearby shopping center offered some prime opportunities.

He tried to peer through the plate glass windows of the businesses lining the sidewalk but couldn't get a clear view of a clock, assuming there were any in this day and age. Everyone had the time on their phones—clocks and watches were fast becoming obsolete.

The sun was shining brightly, making it hard for him to focus, especially after being in a drug-induced, five-day deep sleep.

He came upon a McDonald's and walked inside, taking his place in line.

He looked at the man in front of him and couldn't believe his luck. Hanging halfway out of the man's back pocket was a twenty-dollar bill. The man was holding the hand of a little girl who probably favored him in the face. But for now, all Kevin could see was his back.

People with children were always the easiest to distract, especially when they were attempting to order a meal in a crowded fast-food restaurant. Everyone standing in line was staring up at the menu boards behind the counter. Who would notice what Kevin was about to do?

Kevin inched closer to the man.

The little girl spoke.

"Daddy, I want chicken nuggets!" she declared as she began to dance and wiggle in line, making her request a song.

"Anything you want, Jasmine." The man smiled as he looked down at the energetic little girl, and just as Kevin had predicted, she favored her father.

"Chicken nuggets, chicken nuggets, chicken nuggets," she chanted playfully. Kevin thought she looked about five.

As she sang and moved, still holding her father's hand, the man stiffened his arm to gain control. The order area was getting crowded.

"Jasmine, do Daddy a favor and sing that song once we have gotten to the table," he suggested. His tone was insistent, letting Jasmine know that now was not the time to play.

The little girl stilled herself with sad eyes that only a moment ago had held excitement.

Jasmine's dance and her father's attempt to control her had managed to knock the twenty- dollar bill out of the man's pocket. This was too easy. Kevin placed his foot on top of the bill and grinned.

Before the line got a chance to move again, Kevin bent down as though he were tying his shoe and removed the twenty-dollar bill from under it, quickly sliding the bill between his sock and sneaker.

Standing upright again, he excused himself from the line and made his way to the exit. And just like that, he was out the door and on the street again, in search of his next victim.

Yes, twenty dollars was enough for him to get what he wanted, but forty dollars would be twice as nice.

Kevin crossed the street so that he was now walking against the flow of foot traffic. He spotted a well-dressed man and bumped into him, reaching his hand into the top pocket of the man's jacket.

"Excuse me," Kevin said lowly.

The man had his head buried in his iPhone and never even acknowledged Kevin.

Kevin smiled triumphantly as he gripped the wallet in his left hand. He slipped into an alley and opened it. Now this was more like it, he thought. The man had one hundred and twenty dollars in twenties in his wallet. Kevin smiled.

He added his new windfall to his sock, tossed the wallet to the ground and resurfaced on the main street. He had no interest in credit cards. They were messy and left a paper trail. Cash was neat and tidy.

Today had been a lucky day, he thought. His shoe was one hundred and forty dollars richer than it was when he had left the flophouse earlier.

He headed back down the street, going a few more blocks before he turned down Meadow Road on his way to Boedeker Street, where he reached a house that stood out from the others—and not in a good way.

He knocked on the door three times.

The door swung open, and his faithful drug dealer, Slick D, looked him square in the eyes with no emotional connection at all.

Kevin spoke first as the tall, dark-skinned man looked at Kevin with disdain, the muscle in his jaw beginning to twitch.

"I have what I owe plus a little bit to get a bit."

Not speaking, Slick D moved from the doorway and allowed Kevin to enter.

Slick D closed the door and turned four locks.

Kevin surveyed the mildly smoky room. A glass-top table displayed a pile of marijuana, a bag of cocaine, some white pills that were probably Xanax, small packs of clear capsules, and small bags of white pebbles.

There were four other men in the barely lit room. Two of the men looked like bodyguards, and their guns were visible. The other two looked like users.

Kevin ignored them all and focused his attention on Slick D.

"Where's my money?" Slick D spoke, his tone low and ominous.

Kevin bent down and pulled all the money from his sock.

Slick D counted it, then walked over to the table and grabbed two of the small baggies. He took a few steps toward Kevin and tossed him the bags.

"You're good with me for now. Don't fuck this up, Kev."

And with that, Kevin turned and headed for the door. One of the bodyguards unlatched the four locks and allowed him to exit.

Kevin walked to the edge of the porch and covered his eyes against the bright sun. He needed a place to go. He thought about the house he'd left and the unconscious bodies that had littered the floor. Not to mention, the couple he'd clocked and knocked out cold.

He stepped off the porch and headed for his destination.

CHAPTER 4

Bianca shuffled the stack of papers with her left hand, supporting her head in her right. She stared at the pages for a few seconds.

"Shit," she said out loud to herself.

She was barely making ends meet. She added up the bills before her, then reversed course and added up her income for that month. She had one hundred and thirty dollars left after all the bills were paid and Vivian was compensated.

Could she survive on that amount of groceries for the month? she wondered.

In that moment, she praised the heavens that the bakery was within walking distance. She was saving a lot of gas money and mileage on her car.

Still thankful that she was able to maintain her home and bakery on the money the bakery pulled in, she took in a deep breath and stuffed the papers inside her bag. She had just stood up from the wooden counter stool when she felt a hand on her shoulder.

"Are you OK? I heard you say 'shit' when I was in the back." It was Vivian.

"Yes, everything is fine." Bianca grabbed the stack of cash that was on the counter and held it out for Vivian. "Here you go!" she said with a smile.

"Thank you!" Vivian said cheerfully, taking the tip money from Bianca.

"We had a pretty great day today," Bianca added.

Vivian headed toward the door, then turned around to face Bianca.

"You don't stay here late to double check everything that I cleaned up, do you?" Vivian joked.

Bianca grabbed her large crossbody bag off the wooden stool, then reached for the second stack of tip money and stuffed it in her bag with the papers. She walked the few steps it took to reach Vivian and smiled.

Vivian cuffed her arm around the inside of Bianca's.

"I am so glad that you aren't staying later than me tonight. I worry about you walking home alone some nights. What would I do if anything happened to the best boss I've ever had?" she joked as she bumped hips with Bianca.

"It's only two blocks. And it's not like I'm walking down any dark alleyways. It's a straight shot." Bianca bumped back and smiled.

They exited the shop, and Bianca broke their embrace to lock up the doors.

"Can I give you a ride? I parked behind the bakery this morning," Vivian added.

"It's only a short walk. I . . ."

Vivian interrupted her before she could go any further. "I am at least going to walk you down one block so that I feel a little better."

"Oh, so this is really all about how you feel and nothing to do with me?" Bianca joked.

Vivian gave her a gentle nudge with her arm and an approving smile. "Of course this is about me. I am the one walking two blocks alone at least four nights a week," Vivian joked sarcastically.

Bianca pouted. "It really is a quick walk."

"Oh, hush, you little brat. I just want you to be more careful."

"I have mace in my purse," Bianca said triumphantly.

"Your purse? That duffel bag on your arm, you mean? By the time you find anything in there you could be captured, stabbed, or anything," Vivian kidded, but there was a slight seriousness in her voice. "Start carrying your mace on one of your belt loops so that it's easy for you to access."

"Yes, Mother! You take such good care of me. I don't know what I would do without you." Bianca's voice had a mildly mocking tone.

When they reached the second corner, they came to a stop. They unlocked arms and hugged.

Vivian spoke. "Be careful, and I'll see you in the morning."

"I promise," Bianca squeezed slightly.

Bianca was grateful to be able to walk the last block alone. She enjoyed taking the short walk after work because it gave her mind some time to unwind.

And today, all she could think about was when Kevin would find his way back to her doorstep. It had been five days since his last visit, and though it was sooner than he usually returned, she still felt herself being slightly hopeful.

She walked the last few steps to the entrance of her duplex community and thought about everything she wanted to do once she got home.

She made her way through the gated area and walked six houses into the community. Absentmindedly, she'd already retrieved her keys from her bag, somehow locating them among everything else that she toted around on a daily basis. She paused for a moment to look around.

Seeing that she was completely alone, she unlocked the front door of her home and quickly stepped inside, turning both locks as soon as she closed the door again. She flipped on the light switch and hung her keys on the hook that was nailed to the wall. She unbuttoned her black slacks and walked down the hallway toward the kitchen. She set her crossbody down on the small island and took off her shoes.

She inhaled a deep breath of relaxation, then walked over to one of the cabinets on the other side of the small island. She reached for a wine glass and headed to the refrigerator to grab the half bottle of chardonnay that was on the door. She walked back to the island and placed both the wine glass and the bottle down. The barely pushed in cork still made a popping sound that echoed through the empty walls of her duplex.

She poured a glass of wine and chose to focus on tiny victories. She had served over two hundred and fifty people today, and she had fully recovered from Kevin's theft and had paid her bakery landlord. All was great in the world, and peace was so close she could taste it.

She took a sip of her wine and allowed her mind to wander. Images of Kevin played like a slideshow.

First, the shabby and pathetic looking version of Kevin flashed in her mind. Then came that body she had glimpsed when he was wearing only his boxers. Next was Clean Kevin, fresh out of the shower and dressed in the clothes that she had set aside for him.

Then came the heartbreaker—the Kevin who used to be. The Kevin before his addiction had taken hold with no intention of letting go. She saw him in a suit, looking sexy and confident. His smile was one that could take her breath away. This image transformed into him standing in their bathroom doorway, beads of water dripping down his chest.

Her eyes opened immediately. She had not even realized that she had closed them. As her vision began to clear, she was brought back to the present.

She looked down at her glass of chardonnay and took a large gulp, shaking her head to will away the memories that plagued her.

She unbuttoned the first three buttons of her purple blouse, and with the glass of wine still in her hand, she headed for her master bedroom. As soon as she entered it, she set her wine glass on the dresser and began to undress completely.

She stepped out of her black slacks and took another sip from her glass of wine. I am in the mood for a bath tonight, she thought.

She walked to the bathroom and turned on the light, pulling back the shower curtain to inspect the tub's cleanliness. She almost always took showers, so the tub was clean enough. She turned on the hot and cold water, adjusting the temperature until it suited her, and allowed the tub to start filling.

Bianca rose to her feet and walked out of the bathroom to her nightstand. She opened the third drawer and removed a package of mixed fragrant flowers. She took the entire bag into the bathroom and sprinkled a handful into the tub. Time for another sip of wine while the tub filled, she thought. She surveyed the glass and decided to head for the kitchen. Once there, she refilled her glass.

When she walked back to her bedroom, the smell of flowers had begun to fill the air. Bianca inhaled deeply, enjoying the scent.

Her tub was nearly full, and the bathroom mirrors were completely steamed over. She set her glass of wine on the bathroom counter and stripped out of her bra and underwear. Then, after retrieving the glass of wine, she lowered herself carefully into the tub.

She looked down at the flowers, watching as they floated and spun around on top of the water, then took another sip of wine. She allowed herself to fully relax. The flowers were a treat for making it through the day, she thought.

Kevin was on her mind now more than usual. She found herself daydreaming of their love making and his sculpted body often. She wanted so badly for him to change back into the man she had married, but as each day passed, Bianca lost more faith that her husband, the man who she loved more than anything else, would ever return.

A tear fell, making a sound in the water that brought her from her thoughts. She held back the rest of the tears that were threatening to follow the first one. Tonight wasn't about Kevin. Tonight, she wanted to reward herself with self-care, but she couldn't even do that without thinking about Kevin.

She could hear her own stern voice inside of her head as she scolded herself. *You didn't put him in the situation he is in, he did, so why are you crying? You had a great day today. Now is not the time to reflect on things you have no control over.*

She took another sip of wine and directed her thoughts away from any ideas of Kevin, and the feeling of relaxation returned.

When her wine glass was finally empty, Bianca set it on the floor close to the bathtub, then plunged her body into the hot water up to her neck. She closed her eyes, not wanting to think about one thing or another. She only inhaled the scent of flowers and allowed herself to enjoy the peace and relaxation that now filled her.

After what seemed like a half hour, the water had finally begun to cool. Bianca scrubbed her body from head to toe with her favorite pink loofah glove and her favorite body wash.

She emerged from the water and wrapped her still dripping wet body in her terry cloth robe before pulling up the tub stopper and exiting the bathroom.

She carried her wine glass to the kitchen and briefly considered stuffing the cork back into the bottle and putting it away in the fridge. Then, changing her mind, she took the bottle back to the bedroom with her, her damp feet leaving dewy footprints on the hardwood floors as she walked.

I might as well enjoy this bottle until the end, she thought, pouring more wine into her glass. There was just one small pour left in the bottle.

She placed both the glass and the bottle on her nightstand and crawled into bed. But before she could get too comfortable, she remembered that her cell phone was still buried in her bag in the kitchen.

"Shit," she said as she scooted herself out of bed. Her cell phone doubled as her alarm clock, and oversleeping was not an option.

She shuffled back to the kitchen and dug through her bag for her smartphone. She pressed the button on the side, and the screen flashed, showing no missed calls or text messages. Odd. She usually got at least a text message from Vivian, she thought as she walked back to her bedroom.

She placed her phone beside the wine glass on her nightstand and found comfort in her bed again, still wrapped only in her robe.

Her phone sounded. A text message appeared on the home screen.

Goodnight, Ms. B. I will see you tomorrow, the message from Vivian read.

Bianca smiled and placed the phone back down on the nightstand. She adored Vivian to the fullest extent.

She picked up her wine glass and drank more, thoroughly enjoying the silence and complete stillness in the air. Sometimes her duplex felt like such a lonely place, but there were also times when she was grateful for the solitude.

Drinking the last of the wine in her glass, she looked over at the bottle and decided against pouring the last glass. She was beginning to feel the effects of the wine, and she certainly couldn't afford to wake up with a headache.

Filled with relaxation and slightly hazy from the chardonnay, she pulled the covers up around her neck and drifted off to sleep without another thought.

CHAPTER 5

When Kevin opened his eyes, he saw his reflection in a full-length mirror. Surprised by his own appearance, he looked around the room and noticed that he was standing in his former master bedroom. He walked around and touched a few things, mesmerized by the sweet scent of vanilla that often filled the room. He breathed in deeply, taking comfort in this distant but fond memory. He closed his eyes to get the full effect of the aroma.

When he opened his eyes again, he turned toward the doorway to see her standing at the bedroom entrance, wearing nothing but one of his navy blue t-shirts that barely grazed her thighs.

He admired his view for a moment, as it had been so long since she had stared at him with such passion in her eyes. He wanted this moment to last for as long as possible, not daring to look away even for a second.

Bianca slowly walked up to him and placed her hand on his chest.

"How was your day at work?" she asked softly.

He looked down at her brown eyes that seemed to sparkle, but when he opened his mouth to speak, no sound came out.

Kevin's eyes squirmed from side to side as his mouth moved but no sound came out.

Bianca continued talking, as if her question had been answered.

"Well, I am glad that you're happy and doing what you love. My day at the bakery was slow. I will be glad when the bakery has finally started to drum up some real business. I love my regulars, but it would be nice to be able to take care of my bakery on my own budget so you wouldn't have to help me with the rent and utilities."

"Don't worry, baby. Everything will be fine. You just wait. You are going to have a line around the block once everyone gets a taste of your pastries and the word gets out," he heard himself say as he opened his arms to accept her now pouting face and realized it was a moment from the past.

Kevin had the same collection of dreams on countless nights. This was one of his favorites because it didn't include fighting with Bianca, yelling and screaming back and forth. Those dreams left him with a feeling of regret when he awoke from them. But not this dream. In this dream, he looked down at his wife and gripped her tightly in his embrace.

She looked up at him from his chest with a smile, then, just like she always did, she stepped back so that Kevin's hands could find the hem of the t-shirt she was wearing. He lifted it above her head, revealing her nakedness except for the cozy purple socks she wore on her feet.

Kevin caressed her cheek as he admired every inch of her body from her toes to her head. His eyes landed on the glimmer in her eyes that seemed to capture his soul. He bent down and pressed his lips against hers, tasting the familiar sweetness.

Like a well-rehearsed dance, their kisses deepened, and Kevin could feel the reach of her arms wrapping around his neck. He bent down and lifted her entire body. She locked her legs around his waist, her arms finally finding a comfortable place around his neck. Kevin cupped his hands under her ass and gripped tightly, squeezing in time with his pulse.

Bianca broke their lips and unsnapped the first two buttons on his shirt, exposing his neck. She kissed his neck as Kevin walked backward until they reached the side of the bed.

With Kevin's calves pressed against the bed, he let himself fall backward, still clutching Bianca. She planted another kiss on his lips before climbing up his body and coming to a stop with her knees on each side of his head.

She pressed her vagina against his face, and he began to devour her. Kevin enjoyed the taste of her sweetness as she began to move back and forth on his mouth, moaning softly.

Kevin's excitement built, driving him to move his tongue around sharply, pushing it in and out of her now dripping wet cave. The more vigorous he became, the harder Bianca began to rock. Her thighs began to shake, signaling that her climax was approaching. Kevin grabbed her ass and pushed her down harder into his face as she grinded.

"Oh yes, baby! It feels so good," her voice sounded as she gripped the comforter surrounding them with both of her hands.

Kevin's response was muffled, and the buzzing of his lips only made her rock harder as her climax was close to explosion.

With a shout, her orgasm finally came, her grip on the comforter loosened, and she was out of breath as though she had sprinted around the block.

Kevin moved his body to the side and lowered her gently so that she was lying next to him. He sat up with his face glistening with her fresh juices and took off his suit jacket and tossed it to the floor. Looking down at her, he continued to unbutton his shirt until he reached his belt buckle.

He unbuckled his belt and unfastened his pants, then stood to undress himself completely by the bed. Bianca laid there naked, watching his every move with adoring eyes but not saying a word.

Once he was down to his boxers and gray tank undershirt, he climbed back onto the bed, placing his body on top of Bianca's.

He kissed her deeply, and they both enjoyed the taste of her sweetness on his lips.

Underneath him, Bianca opened her legs as they kissed. Her arms came up and wrapped around his neck as she clung to him in all her nakedness. Their kisses deepened, and he felt his hardness reach its maximum extension.

Bianca loosened her legs and scooted her body down more on the bed to receive him.

Sitting up to pull out his rock hardness from his boxers, he stared down at her adoringly for a few seconds, then watched as her face turned into a pleasurable expression as he slowly inserted himself inside the wetness that her orgasm had created.

Kevin couldn't hold back his own moan from the warmth that readily accepted him. Sliding in and out, back and forth, he teased them both. A light shudder went through Bianca as he moved in and out of her slowly and intentionally with every stroke.

Both of them began to pant in pleasure.

Kevin started to lose his ability to concentrate on slow strokes, and his pace sped up slightly. The change in pace caused Bianca to begin to moan louder in pleasure.

Excited by the sound of her moaning, Kevin's pace increased more. This time, Bianca's hips began to meet his, pushing against his rhythm with force. Kevin knew that she was on her way to another climax, so he matched her rhythm and vigor.

Wrapping her arms around his back, she clung to him as she released her second orgasm with a heavy breath. Her body went limp.

Kevin smirked because he wasn't quite finished with her yet. He sat up and tapped her legs, even though her eyes were closed.

Still out of breath, chest moving up and down, her eyes opened slowly.

Kevin held out his finger and made a turnaround motion.

Bianca sat up and got on all fours in front of him.

Kevin slapped her ass, and she moaned in excitement and anticipation. He entered her from behind without hesitation, setting a pace that was fast and persistent as he moved in and out of her.

Bianca's voice sounded immediately. "Yes, baby! It feels so good!" she shouted.

He slapped her ass in response and grabbed her hips as he plunged in deeper.

"Oh yes! That's the spot!"

He could feel her muscles began to tighten again, and his grin became more devious as he could feel her walls beginning to pulsate, signaling that another orgasm was on its way. The warmth inside of her turned to hotness, and Kevin could feel his own climax approaching. It was his turn to speak.

"God damn, baby! This pussy is so good! I . . ."

Before he could get another word out, he could feel her wetness increasing due to her last and final orgasm, and it caused him to release his own climax inside of her with a loud deep groan of pleasure.

Unable to hold her body with her limbs, she collapsed forward. Kevin followed suit and dropped down beside her in their bed.

He stared into her half-open eyes as she smiled.

Waking up from his hazy dream, Kevin came back to reality. He found himself sitting on the floor, his back against the wall in a filthy bedroom with a dirty mattress that he was glad was empty, grateful to be in solitude.

He stumbled to his feet, trying to shake off the headache that immediately began to throb once he stood. He stumbled forward four or five steps, and his legs bumped the bed.

He turned toward the closed door and forced his legs to keep moving. He grabbed the doorknob and exited, relieved that the hallway contained just one person, curled up in a ball at the far end of the hall.

With the pounding headache he had, he was glad that no one else was awake. He walked down the hallway with his hand on his head.

As he passed the living room area, he kept his eyes on the front door, not looking left or right. As long as he wasn't disturbed, he couldn't care less about the junkies who hovered in the abandoned house looking for their next fix.

He pitied these people. They needed more self-control. When he was ready to give this shit up for good, he knew that he could without question. I just don't have an addictive personality, he thought.

He grabbed the door handle as he shook his head in shame and exited the house into the dark of night.

The night looked extremely different from the day. There were actually more people walking the streets now, as if the monsters had come out to play and Kevin was invited. He looked down at himself to gauge his cleanliness.

This determined where he could roam at night. His headache kept him from wanting to get into any scuffles. He just wanted easy prey so that there would be no need for violence.

He was semi-clean; he'd certainly looked worse, he thought as he looked down at his dark gray t-shirt that had a few crusty stains. His black jeans had some dark stains that were visible up close, but he doubted anyone else would notice. He thought about Bianca.

He quickly decided against going to her house. His last incident was still too fresh in his mind. He had to wait until the memory had faded and she would be happy to see him again. Kevin knew taking the money was wrong, but he was desperate and he knew it.

He knew, like always, that she would find a way to replace it. He had needed it to pay off a debt and save his ass. Kevin hated that he had to steal from the woman he loved, but it was a risk he was willing to take, even if it meant hurting them both. Kevin wasn't willing to be beaten or lose a limb over money. He paid his debts in full and at all costs.

He remembered the present moment and looked around just as a group of three guys passed him in the night, each of them nodding separately.

The night was like heaven to Kevin. Darkness afforded the perfect cover, and drunks were easy marks. He walked down the street with purpose; he knew exactly where he was headed.

There was a strip of bars about eighteen blocks away. Kevin took that long walk in stride, nodding casually and confidently at passersby.

After about fifteen minutes, Kevin found himself surrounded by the buzz of the city. The nightlife was busy, and Kevin was glad to see so many distracted people. He spotted his first victim and directed his attention toward her.

She stumbled slightly as she walked down the street, in deep conversation on her phone. The flap of her purse hung open. Kevin walked past the young woman, who looked about twenty-five, and bumped into her.

"Excuse me," he mumbled, without looking at her directly, and grabbed her wallet. She only glanced briefly in his direction and went back to her conversation.

The streets were busy, and bumps happened. Easy prey, he thought as he gripped the wallet in his hand and opened it quickly, taking out the money and dumping the wallet in the closest trash can. No one around him even noticed. He stuffed the money in the pocket of his jeans and continued down the street. Time for another victim.

Perfect, he thought. He had spotted a man on the other side of the street, drunkenly attempting to chat up a woman.

Kevin crossed the street with the rest of the throng in the crosswalk and gave the staggering man a bump as he pulled the wallet from the man's back pocket.

The key to being a successful thief and staying out of jail was knowing when to stop, and Kevin opted to be satisfied with the money he'd already collected. The night was still fairly young, but why risk getting caught?

He felt the wad of money in his jeans and thought about Bianca. He walked aimlessly, deep in thought. Before he realized it, he was standing in front of her duplex.

He stared at the light on in her living room, looking for any movement. He caught a quick glimpse of her passing by the window and smiled, wondering what she was doing.

Kevin flashed back to his memories of her moving about in the duplex they had once shared, straightening throw pills, picking up misplaced shoes, cooking meals, and gathering up laundry.

He remembered how he would playfully scold her and tell her to sit down and relax before pulling her to the couch and tickling her into submission.

How he missed those times. Seemed like a lifetime ago, he thought. He stood outside for about forty-five minutes until her light went off. Then he resumed his walk in the night.

When he reached an alley, he stopped briefly to count the two bundles of cash he'd stolen, using the light from a streetlamp above.

The first bundle contained two hundred and twenty dollars in an assortment of bills, ranging from ones to twenties. Big spender! Kevin thought, folding the stack and putting it back in his jeans. That drunkard must have been planning to buy rounds of drinks all night. He was going to have a rude awakening when he reached for his wallet.

Kevin pulled out the second wad, hoping for another surprisingly large windfall. After all, the young woman had been dripping in expensive looking clothing. His face curled up when he realized that the wad of cash contained mostly ones and fives. Tip money, perhaps, he thought. He shrugged his shoulders and shoved the money into his jeans.

Kevin estimated that he had at least three hundred, maybe even three-fifty. He knew that if he played his cards right he'd be set for the next few days.

Kevin's stomach grumbled in hunger. He couldn't remember the last time he had eaten. Getting a score would have to wait.

Up ahead, the William's Chicken sign beckoned to him, and his mouth began to water.

"Well, I might as well eat," he said as he tried to think harder about the last time he had tasted any food on his tongue.

Kevin headed in the direction of the William's Chicken restaurant, which was only a few blocks away. When he got to the corner he made a left. As he walked, he pulled the money from his pockets and began to count it.

Kevin's lips curled into a smile when he finished counting. He had underestimated his stash. Three hundred and sixty-seven dollars wasn't bad for just two people. He was definitely satisfied with his spoils, and the night was still young.

Maybe he would get a room, he thought as he folded the money into one large bundle, placed it in his front pocket, and began to walk, getting closer to his destination.

The smell of chicken was heavy—and heavenly. Kevin nodded his head to the handful of people standing around outside the door and entered.

There were only a few people inside. One man was waiting for his order at the counter. A couple on one side of the restaurant seemed to be doing more talking than eating, while a man on the other side of the restaurant was leaning over his chicken dinner, eating with gusto.

Kevin stood behind the man in line and waited his turn. After only a minute or two, he reached the counter and ordered a four-piece dark with fries, corn fritters, and two peppers to go. He pulled out the bundle of cash.

A few minutes later, a man from the kitchen approached the counter with Kevin's to-go box. They both nodded, and Kevin walked outside with a box of hot food in his hands.

The cool breeze from the night's sky felt refreshing, and he began his brisk walk to his next destination without giving another nod to the folks gathered outside. As he walked down the street, the smell of the chicken was tantalizing. The Ramada Inn was only a few blocks away.

He entered the lobby and walked up to the counter where a dark-skinned woman with a little too much makeup and a straight-haired black wig was working.

She looked up when she saw him approaching the counter and smiled, batting her eyes slightly and revealing red lipstick smudges on her white teeth.

"What can I do for you, handsome?" Her tone had the note of a different meaning.

"Room for one, king-sized bed, nonsmoking." He smiled back at the woman, who wore a name tag that said Tanya.

There was a spark in her eyes when she saw his smile, and her smile widened to reveal a small chip in her front tooth.

"That will be eighty-three dollars."

Kevin pulled the wad of cash from his jeans and counted out the money. When he handed her the money their hands touched for a second. Tanya's face turned slightly red.

"Thank you."

Accepting his cash, she pulled out a key card from a nearby drawer and scanned it on the card reader, placed it inside a white paper sleeve, and handed it to Kevin. Their hands brushed briefly again and their eyes locked.

"Please let me know if there is anything else you need tonight." Her voice was sultry.

Kevin smiled and accepted the key card from Tanya's hand.

He looked down at the paper covering the key card and read the room number: 325. He walked in the direction of the elevator, holding the box of chicken.

Once he stepped into the elevator, he thought about the hot shower and warm bed that awaited him and smiled.

It was going to feel so good to eat a good meal, get a good night's rest, and take a hot shower. He couldn't wash his clothes, but he could at least rinse them out and let them hang dry. His shirt was beginning to get dingy, and his boxers had definitely seen better days.

He stepped off the elevator and walked down the hall in the direction of his room. For tonight, the Ramada Inn was home.

CHAPTER 6

The last few days had gone by so quickly, Bianca thought as she wiped down the bakery counter. She had finally remembered to have a key made for Vivian, and that had brought her a wave of relief. With her bakery's popularity growing, she didn't want another mishap like the morning when she was late because of her missing money to cause her to lose customers.

It was midday, and a few of the regulars had stopped by for a sandwich and some of Bianca's fresh-made fries. It was the only lunch special Bianca offered—the sandwich of the day and fries—and almost everyone indulged in a pastry for dessert.

She smiled at her intimate group of lunch customers.

Vivian walked behind her carrying a tray, playfully bumping into her as she spoke.

"What has you smiling so wide?" she asked with a curious voice.

"Oh, nothing. Just loving the mild success of my new lunch special." She spun around to face Vivian, who had put down the tray and stood with one hand on her hip.

Before Vivian could comment, the bell on the front door sounded its familiar jingle, letting them know that someone had entered the bakery.

Both women's eyes lit up at the sight of the handsome, dark-skinned man in the doorway. His expression shifted from serious to a perfect smile when he noticed that their eyes were on him. His build was nice—not too slim and not too big. His muscular physique was visible under black slacks and a dark olive button-up shirt with silver buttons.

Bianca spoke before Vivian did. "Good afternoon! Welcome to Pastries From Paradise! Would you like to try our lunch special?" She smiled big enough for her teeth to show.

The man waited until he reached the counter before he spoke, his voice was deep and raspy. There was a sense of authority in his presence.

"I came with a taste for a cinnamon roll, but please tell me more about this lunch special." He locked eyes with Bianca and sat directly in front of her.

"We have the buffalo chicken BLT with spinach on rye, my home-style seasoned fries, and a glass of sweet tea."

"That sounds delicious." His eyes locked with hers again. "I would love to see and taste what you have to offer." Was it her imagination, or was there a double meaning in his response?

Breaking their eye contact, Bianca panicked and turned around, begging with her eyes for help. Vivian quickly approached the counter with a smile of her own.

"Sounds great. We will get your lunch ready as soon as we can," Vivian said.

"My name is Michael." He looked at Vivian and then at the back of Bianca's head. She was prepping some of the fries.

"Well, Michael, you won't be disappointed," Vivian assured him.

He took his eyes away from Bianca and looked at Vivian. "With as beautiful as you two ladies are, disappointment is the last thing on my mind." His eyes went back to Bianca.

Vivian chuckled and walked away to pour his sweet tea, leaving him to stare uninterrupted.

Bianca removed her special fries from the deep fryer and set them aside to drain while she prepared his sandwich. She plated his food and grabbed the cup of sweet tea that Vivian had poured.

"Enjoy," she said with a smile, placing the food and tea on the counter in front of Michael.

"Oh, I plan to." He looked at her and then at the fresh lunch she had prepared for him.

Bianca walked away and pulled a fresh cloth from under the counter and began wiping down the opposite side of the bar. It was her attempt to keep her focus off of the attractive man and on her business.

"That's not fair."

Bianca stopped wiping the counter and looked up at his words.

"You know my name, but I have no idea what your name is." He searched the front of her pastel pink dress for a name tag.

Noticing his body search, Bianca started wiping the counter again before she spoke.

"My name is Bianca. I am the owner of Pastries From Paradise. A name tag isn't necessary."

"Well, Bianca, can I get a refill?"

Michael held up his half-empty glass and shook it so that the ice clanked together.

Bianca stopped cleaning and took the glass from Michael. And this time, when their hands brushed, Bianca felt a spark that made her take a step back.

Michael smiled at her reaction.

Bianca looked down at his plate instead of his eyes and noticed that his sandwich was half-eaten, and he only had a few fries left.

Michael's eyes moved in the direction of her eyes.

"This was such an unexpected treat. Being served a delicious meal by a ravishingly beautiful woman. I think I have found my place in heaven," he grinned.

Her eyes moved from his plate to his eyes.

"I'm glad you enjoyed it," she smiled.

"Oh, I'm not finished yet. When this plate is clean, and you've brought out one of those freshly glazed cinnamon rolls, my life will be complete."

She laughed as casually as she could and placed the freshly refilled glass in front of him.

"I am sincerely glad that everything is to your liking. Every day we offer a different sandwich for the lunch special. Tomorrow's special will be a mozzarella pizza grilled cheese, so feel free to drop in again for lunch."

"I will make sure that I do," he smiled.

And with that, Bianca went back to tidying up the bar. "Let me know when you're ready for that cinnamon roll," she added.

"I am starting to have a taste for something sweet, but it's definitely not the cinnamon roll," she heard him say when her back was turned. She could sense his grin.

"I'm sorry. Did you say something?" She turned around, finding the courage to look him the eyes.

His eyes challenged her. "I said I am sure that cinnamon roll will be exceptionally sweet." He looked her up and down, and again she felt his double meaning.

Bianca blushed and broke their eye contact. "I am positive it will be gratifying. What did you say your name was?" she joked.

"I'm hurt. You've forgotten my name already?" Michael pouted playfully. "This cinnamon roll had better be on the house."

Bianca put her hand on her chin, as though she were thinking. "Marcus, was it? Mario? Mitchell?" She looked up at the ceiling, as if the right name would be written up there somewhere.

Michael gave her a look with sad puppy eyes, as though his feelings were truly hurt. "Really?" he said in a low tone.

Bianca burst into laughter. She reached her hand out and touched his arm. "Of course, I am just kidding, Michael," she said with a smile.

There was another spark, and she moved her hand away quickly. Now it was his turn to smile.

"This is the second time you've shocked me today. You must be walking static electricity."

"Ha, ha. No, it's you who's been shocking me. One more time, and I'll be forced to make a police report for the bodily harm you caused," she joked.

"Oh, you have jokes! I will do you some bodily harm all right. Just let me get close enough."

The last part of his sentence trailed off in silence.

Hearing his every word, Bianca folded her arms across her chest. She was suddenly very uncomfortable.

"So, what's that supposed to mean?" she asked, on the verge of anger.

"Let me take you out for dinner, and I'll be more than happy to show you."

She blushed and added, "There will be no dates for me considering I am married."

Michael searched her hands for a ring that wasn't there, but a faint band line was still visible on her left ring finger.

"Some wife you are! Walking around with no band on."

"That situation is more complicated than you know and none of your business, Mr. Michael."

"Well, excuse me for being curious about such a beautiful woman, and one I find particularly interesting."

"Keep your interest to yourself, Mr. Michael. That is definitely where it belongs."

Relieved that another customer had walked in, Bianca stepped away.

"Good afternoon, ma'am. It's a beautiful day here at Pastries From Paradise. How can I make your day just a little bit sweeter?" It was one of Bianca's favorite ways to greet a customer.

The woman smiled and eagerly ordered.

Bianca looked over and winked at Michael to let him know there were no hard feelings. He was watching the exchange intently.

Bianca began to circulate through the room, offering refills and extra napkins, and delivering freshly made lunch specials. She stayed busy, and after about thirty minutes, she noticed that Michael was missing from his spot at the counter.

Good. He was finally gone, she thought, feeling relieved that there would be no more awkward banter—at least for today.

She walked over to the bar top, where his empty plate and glass sat. As soon as she lifted the plate, she saw a napkin with a note on it.

I will be back, beautiful. I definitely want to get to know the woman behind this adorable bakery. Can't wait for tomorrow's lunch special. He had signed with a winking smile and the letter M.

After reading the note, Bianca crumbled it in her hand.

Vivian came up behind her, noticing that she had begun to stare off into space.

"What's got you daydreaming?" she asked.

"Michael is planning to return. I haven't decided if that's a good or bad thing." She handed Vivian the crumbled note.

"Ooh, honey. It looks like you have an admirer and a fine one at that," Vivian smirked playfully.

"You hush. I have enough going on without dealing with a damn admirer." Bianca bumped hips with Vivian to move her out of the way as she carried the plate and other dishes to the sink. She laughed to herself as she started to load the plates from the lunch rush into the dishwasher.

"If you say so," Vivian said as she grabbed the broom resting on a nearby wall and began to sweep.

CHAPTER 7

The next day, Michael returned. But he chose a table not too far away from the counter so that he was in full view of Bianca.

Vivian took his order as Bianca served another customer from behind the counter.

"What can I get for you?" Vivian said with a smile.

"Whatever the special is for the day," Michael smiled back, looking past Vivian at Bianca working behind the counter.

"Coming right up," Vivian said cheerfully.

Once Michael's order was done, Bianca chose to take it out to him. No sense in trying to avoid him, she thought.

"I see you kept your word and decided to join us for lunch again today."

"How could I resist something so delicious?" He looked at the food, then looked her up and down.

She blushed and set the plate on the table in front of him. "Enjoy your meal," she added, walking off.

"Oh, I plan to," she heard him say as she put more distance between them.

Once she reached the counter, she felt like she could breathe again. She exhaled with so much force that she drew the attention of a customer three seats away.

Bianca smiled and nodded, conveying that everything was fine without saying a word.

Still smiling, she walked around the counter and busied herself with wiping off counters and stacking dishes in the sink, making sure not to look up, knowing that Michael was watching her every move.

Hearing the faintest "excuse me," Bianca looked up into the eyes of the woman who'd noticed Bianca's deep breathing just moments ago.

"May I have more coffee?" the woman asked, smiling warmly.

Returning her smile, Bianca grabbed the coffee pot and approached the woman to pour her a refill.

"I apologize for the wait. It seems my lunch special was a hit, and we are a little busier than usual," Bianca said with pride as she looked around the small seating area. Only two tables out of eight were available.

"This sandwich was soo delicious," the woman said, taking the last bite of her mozzarella pizza grilled cheese sandwich.

"I'm glad you enjoyed it." Bianca's smile doubled in size as she grabbed an extra napkin and placed it in front of the woman before leaving her to her fresh coffee.

As she turned to go back to cleaning, she met Vivian coming behind the counter.

"How's it going with Mr. Sexy?" Vivian asked playfully.

"I think I held my breath the entire time he talked to me. I made it back in one piece," Bianca said, jokingly wiping fake sweat from her brow.

Vivian giggled. "There's nothing wrong with a little innocent flirting, Ms. B. He is fine and seems into you. I say flirt away and then go home feeling good."

Vivian smiled, folding her arms in triumph.

As they both turned toward the counter, Michael approached, taking their attention.

"I wasn't sure if I was supposed to leave the plate on the table or bring it here," he said, holding the plate out for one of them to grab.

Bianca's hand reached out first. Taking the plate, she spoke. "Thank you, but you could've left it on the table."

"And leave without saying goodbye?" When he spoke, he made sure he held eye contact with her.

There was a brief silence when no one made a sound.

Feeling the awkwardness that was beginning to build, Vivian spoke. "Enjoy the rest of your day, Michael. We'll see you tomorrow."

Michael released the plate and broke eye contact, snapping Bianca from her trance.

"See you around the same time tomorrow," Bianca said after he had turned around to leave, finally able to find her voice.

"It's a date," he said as he opened the door and walked out.

Neither of them spoke again until the door had completely closed.

"Well, I'll be damned. Someone may have more than a little crush," Vivian pointed out.

"I can admit he is very fine, and I can't predict how things will turn out with me and Kevin, but I can't even think about another man in my current situation. Yes, flirting or almost flirting is great, but it's only flirting to get me through another day. At the end of the day, Kevin is where my loyalty lies."

Vivian didn't dare respond to Bianca's statement, even if she did have an opinion. They were good friends, but Bianca was still the boss. Vivian grabbed the broom and continued to sweep behind the counter.

At that moment, a customer sitting patiently signaled for some assistance.

"What can I do for you ma'am?" Bianca asked.

The woman's sandwich was nearly finished, and her glass was empty.

"Do you have orange juice or cranberry juice?"

"We have both. Which one would you prefer?"

The woman thought for a second. "Cranberry juice," she said with finality.

"Coming right up," Bianca bubbled.

She enjoyed these everyday interactions with her customers—that's what running a business was all about, and Bianca was a natural at making customers feel catered to and welcome. And speaking of customers . . .

Bianca had to admit that she enjoyed Michael's attention. She liked that he instinctively watched every step and move that she made—as if it were habit and not even slightly predatory—and that intrigued her. In the time that she had been separated from Kevin, many men had attempted to approach her, and she had been able to gracefully send them away. But somehow this felt different. Only two days had passed, and she was uncharacteristically falling all over herself and holding her breath when he smiled. She shook away the thoughts and focused on pouring the woman's cranberry juice.

"Please feel free to let me know if there is anything else you need," Bianca said kindly, setting the glass on the table in front of the woman.

Bianca was glad she had taken a chance and opened a business she was passionate about. She was also glad that word of mouth regarding her lunch specials had spread like wildfire, and she hoped that one day soon she wouldn't have to juggle her finances so carefully. She needed to build up some savings for a rainy day.

"It was great to have you. Please come again," she called as a few people departed.

Bianca looked up at the antique clock on the wall.

It was almost four o'clock in the afternoon, two hours from closing time. She took another survey of the room and saw a couple of people still deep in conversation and clearly not leaving any time soon. Bianca looked back at Vivian, who was staring at her, reading Bianca's thoughts.

"Today was a really great day. How many lunch specials did you make?"

Bianca pretended to count on her fingers.

Vivian smiled, knowing that Bianca knew exactly how many lunch specials she had made. Vivian looked down at her invisible watch and tapped it, signaling that her time was running out with this calculation.

"I would say anywhere from ten to fifteen."

"That's a few more than yesterday. Looks like you found your customer driver," Vivian said, pulling a wrapped sandwich from beneath the counter. She unwrapped it slowly, as though it might be delicate and took a bite. Her eyes closed in pleasure. "This is heaven on a plate."

Bianca laughed. "I saved that sandwich just for you."

"What are you eating, Ms. B?"

"I nibbled here and there so I'm good."

Bianca moved around the counter as Vivian ate, collecting a few dishes from empty tables and feeling grateful.

It was five thirty before the place had cleared out and all the dirty dishes were loaded into the dishwasher.

A job well done, Bianca thought.

Vivian tried one more time to gauge Bianca's feelings about Michael. "So what do you really think about Mr. Sexy?"

Bianca sighed. "I think as long as he keeps coming in here I'm going to flirt with him, but it will definitely not go beyond that, simply because I don't want it to."

"Well, I say flirt away, honey. There's no harm in that. Just be careful. I always want you to be safe out here. You never know when Kevin's going to walk through that door and say he's ready for rehab and to start again. That's what I hope for the most. You two were my favorite couple. But in the meantime, harmlessly flirt with the hot guy who can't stop staring at you. I could barely take his order. I might as well be invisible because he looked right past me. I know I'm fine, but that made me slightly jealous," Vivian smirked.

Bianca rolled her eyes as she cleaned up the kitchen, not taking Vivian's bait.

CHAPTER 8

Kevin woke up and almost forgot where he was. The mattress and sheets smelled fresh. The room was clean and didn't reek of mildew and dirty socks. He was alone. He sat up in the bed and oriented himself. He was at the Ramada Inn.

He wiped the sleep from his eyes and smiled. At least something had gone his way for a change.

He got to his feet and took a long, hard stretch. It struck him how tired he still was. Looking down at what he had fallen asleep in, he began to disrobe until there was nothing left to take off. He grabbed the clothes from the floor and headed straight for the closet. Thankful that there was a robe—very cheaply made but a robe nonetheless.

He considered his options for washing his clothes. He could find a place within walking distance and wash his clothes there; he could call the front desk and find out if there was a laundry service; or he could walk to the nearest convenience store, grab some detergent, hand wash everything, and hang everything out to dry. But that last option would take way too long.

Kevin picked up the phone and pressed zero to get the front desk.

"Thank you for choosing the Ramada Inn! This is Tanya. Can I help you with some room service today?"

Hearing her voice, Kevin envisioned the woman who had checked him in the night before.

"Yes, this is the guest in room 325. I was wondering if you did laundry."

Recognizing his voice, she softened her pitch. "Why yes we do, handsome."

He could practically hear her smiling through the phone.

"Someone will be up to your room in a few moments to pick up your belongings, and we'll have them back to you in an hour."

She spoke again after only a few seconds of silence. "Was there something else you needed?" It was an innocent question, but it was tinged with a double entendre.

"No, but thank you," he said as he smiled into the phone.

"Call down if you think of anything. Remember that checkout is at eleven."

Kevin looked at the clock on the nightstand and saw that it was nine thirty.

"Thank you, beautiful," he flirted innocently.

"You're welcome." He could hear the smile in her voice again, and then the line disconnected.

Kevin noticed that he was still gripping his filthy clothes in his arm and walked over to the door, dropping the clothes on the floor. He headed back to bed and did something he never got to do. He grabbed the remote and turned on the TV.

He had only flipped through four channels before he heard a knock at the door.

"Room service," a woman's voice announced.

He walked to the door and picked up his clothes before opening it. He was surprised to see Tanya standing in front of him.

He looked her up and down. She wore a black blazer, blue shirt, and gray slacks that hugged her form perfectly.

Kevin could feel his manhood rising to attention. Her body looked much more appealing than her overly made-up face.

"The maid was busy so I came up instead," she offered as an explanation for her presence.

"Thank you for such personal service." He smiled as he handed her his clothes.

She grabbed them and their arms brushed.

"Would you like to come inside?" His question just popped out before he had a chance to think about it.

"I was wondering what took you so long to ask. I thought maybe if I came up you would finally get the hint."

She breezed past him into the room and dropped his clothes in a corner. She removed her blazer as he closed the door.

Kevin walked up and assisted her, unbuttoning her slacks and sliding both her pants and panties down over her nicely rounded ass until they fell to the floor.

No one spoke.

She unhooked her bra through her shirt and pulled both over her head. She stepped forward out of her panties and pants.

Kevin stepped back to give her some room, and she dropped to her knees.

Parting his robe, she took him into her mouth completely, causing him to gasp. As her head moved back and forth, Kevin's eyes closed tightly. He enjoyed the pleasure and warmth of her wet mouth.

She moaned when he grabbed the back of her head, forcing his erection deeper into her mouth. She increased her speed until he pulled himself away, not wanting to explode in her mouth. She rose to her feet, waiting for his next move.

He reveled at the sight of her body, then threw her onto the bed and began to devour her center.

She moaned in ecstasy as she gripped the sheets of the unmade bed.

She tasted surprisingly sweet, causing Kevin to deepen his efforts.

"Oh yes, baby. Just like that." Her voice was raspy.

The encouragement only stoked Kevin's efforts.

"Oh yes, baby. I'm about to cum!" she exclaimed, her voice a high pitch that rang in the room.

Enjoying the flavor, he awaited her climax, his tongue moving in all directions. Once he could feel her juices flowing, he arose from his position with a glistening face. Wiping his mouth with his hand, he grabbed his rock hard manhood and stroked it a few times, preparing to insert it into the fountain he had just created.

She opened her legs invitingly.

He entered her with force, and they both gasped in instant pleasure. He started his pace slowly at first, making every stroke intentional.

Like her mouth, Tanya's warm paradise began to increase in moisture, and he could feel her climax beginning to build. Teasing her, he pulled completely out and tapped his manhood on her clit, causing her to squirm and whimper. He wasn't ready for her to climax yet.

It had been weeks—probably even a month—since Kevin had been given such a privilege, and he planned on selfishly enjoying bringing this woman to the point of insanity just because he could. He thought about his last dream and inserted his dick back into Tanya, who moaned as soon as he entered her.

This time his pace was quicker. He looked down at her quivering body and smirked.

Unable to take the deepened stroke, Tanya climaxed again, this time with a shout.

This had encouraged Kevin's climax, and he pulled out suddenly, spraying her body with semen with a low groan. He was grateful for the release that he hadn't even realized he missed.

Tanya laid there, covered in semen, still attempting to catch her breath.

Sitting back on his legs, Kevin relaxed and wiped the sweat from his brow with the sheet.

Tanya sat up in the bed on her elbows.

"I must say, that was better than I was expecting," she said, her smile bigger than he had ever seen it.

"I enjoyed you too. Shit was good as fuck." Kevin got off the bed.

Tanya got up from the bed and went to the bathroom and turned on the shower.

Kevin was beginning to see the steam coming from the shower.

Tanya popped her head out and spoke. "Are you joining me or were you planning to stay out there?" Her head popped back inside once he took his first steps toward the bathroom.

After they fucked in the shower once more and washed their bodies, Kevin put his robe back on and watched as Tanya dressed back in her work clothes. She fixed her hair and grabbed his laundry.

An hour and a half had passed, leaving Kevin just fifteen minutes until checkout.

When she reached the door, he spoke. "Does this mean I can forget about checkout time?"

"You stay right here. You can check out after our next two rounds. I get off at eight." Her voice was sultry when she spoke, and Kevin heard the door close behind her.

Kevin laid back in the bed and relaxed, deciding if he actually wanted to stay here until eight or if he would take advantage of the extra time and leave when he felt like it. He thought about the money he had spent and what he had left. He thought about going to make a run to see Slick D. Then he thought about the abandoned house that he got high in.

Unable to make a decision, he grabbed the remote, turned on the television, and began flipping through the channels.

Not realizing that he had fallen asleep, Kevin woke up with the remote still in his hand. He looked up at the television to see an old western movie playing. As Gabby Hayes made his appearance across the screen, Kevin's eyes moved to the clock on the nightstand. It was one thirty in the afternoon.

At that moment, there was a knock at the door. Still groggy, Kevin stumbled to the door, hearing an unfamiliar voice call out, "Room Service!"

This time when he opened the door, he saw a short, older Hispanic woman with strawberry red hair. She couldn't have been much over five feet tall, and she wore a light gray maid uniform. When the door opened, she smiled, holding the folded clothes in a stack in both hands.

"Here you are, *señor*. Nice clean clothes."

Accepting the clothes in one hand, Kevin smiled before he spoke. "Gracias." His Spanish accent definitely needed work.

"De nada." She nodded her head in approval and began to walk away from the door.

He waited a few seconds before he allowed the door to swing shut.

Coming back into the room, Kevin threw the clothes on the end of the bed and started going over his plans for the rest of his day. He felt his stomach growl, and he realized that he hadn't eaten anything since the chicken the night before.

Just then, there was a second knock on the door. This time, Kevin knew it was Tanya coming back for more. But when he opened the door, he was surprised to see a young man holding a tray.

Kevin looked at the young man in confusion.

"Room service, sir," he said, handing Kevin a small white card.

Here's some lunch on me to help replenish some of that energy from earlier. Have this for now. I'll be up later. Tanya

Looking up from the note, Kevin accepted the tray from the young man. He was dressed in a crisp, black button-down and perfectly creased khaki pants. His name tag said Derek.

Kevin accepted the food tray and stepped back into the room. The food's aroma hit his nose, and his stomach made another sound.

He walked to the bed and lifted the cover off of the plate of food. He was delighted to see fried pork chops and gravy, with mashed potatoes and a small cup of broccoli.

His mouth began to water, and though it was completely uncharacteristic of him, he found himself at the phone pressing zero to get the front desk.

"Thank you for choosing the Ramada Inn. This is Tanya. How can I help you?"

"Thank you for the lunch, baby." His voice was deep and seductive. He imagined her smile through the phone.

"I need you energized for what I have in store for you later."

Kevin sighed in response.

"What's wrong, baby?" she questioned.

"I have some other errands today. Can I get a raincheck?"

Now it was her turn to sigh. "When will I see you again?"

"I'll come by and get your card from you before I leave. I don't have a number you can call, but I'll make sure I find a way to reach you."

"You don't have a number I can call?" she asked, her tone suspicious.

"No, sweetheart. But I am a man of my word. As sexy as that body of yours is, I definitely want to see it a few more times," he flirted to reassure her.

"Enjoy the meal, and I'll see you next time," she said skeptically.

"You sure will." Kevin wasn't sure of anything at all, but he wanted to keep this particular door open.

With that, he heard the line click and placed the phone back on the receiver so that he could dig into his delicious feast.

Later, standing in front of the hotel room's full-length mirror, Kevin observed his cleanliness. With the way things were starting off today, it was shaping up to be a great one.

He smiled and looked himself up and down. The dark gray t-shirt had lines in it where the maid had creased it, and his jeans had a similar soft crease going down the front of both legs.

The sneakers he wore looked mildly worn, and he was officially satisfied with his appearance.

He had stashed his wad of cash in a dresser drawer, and he pulled it out to recount it. Did he have enough left for a score? Tanya had graced him with a meal, so he didn't have to worry about food.

He counted two hundred and eighty-four dollars and stuffed it in his pocket. Plenty for a couple of scores and another night in a hotel if he wanted. He walked back to the mirror and prepared for his exit. Giving himself another once over, he smiled in approval and grabbed the door handle.

As promised, he headed toward the elevator en route to the front desk.

When Tanya saw him come from around the corner, her face lit up with excitement.

He casually walked up to the counter and greeted her with an inviting smile. "Well, good afternoon, beautiful. Stopping by before I head out."

Her smile quickly changed into a pout. "I was just about to get some lunch and head back upstairs for another round." There was seduction in her voice.

"I have someplace else to be, but we will definitely catch up soon." He grabbed her hand, not sure if he was telling the truth or lying, and stroked it.

Tanya blushed in response to his touch and reached behind the desk with her other hand and pulled out a card.

"Call me when you are in the neighborhood. The room will most definitely be on the house."

She placed the card on the desk and winked at him.

Now it was his turn to smile. He grabbed the card in response. "Well, I will definitely keep that in mind," he said, licking his lips as he walked toward the main doors.

He passed a couple lugging their bags, ready to check in. He greeted them with a smile as he passed.

On the street, the day was pleasant. The sun was shining brightly, and there was a nice breeze that was cool and refreshing to the skin.

Kevin began his walk toward Slick D's. It took fourteen blocks to get to Meadow Road and Boedeker Street. Kevin wasn't in a rush. He casually and calmly walked up to the door and knocked his usual three times.

There was a pause before anyone answered. When the door did open, Kevin was greeted with a cloud of smoke. He inhaled before he stepped forward and entered the house.

"Well, if it isn't my favorite attorney." In rare moments like this one, Slick D welcomed Kevin with open arms and a smile.

Kevin's head lifted and his chest rose as he walked across the room, feeling as though this was the treatment he should've always been receiving.

Slick D walked him over to a black marble table that was covered in an assortment of small bags. Each cluster of bags looked as though it contained something different. Kevin's eyes locked on small zip lock bags that each contained five clear capsules. He could feel his excitement building.

Slick D was talking and patting Kevin on his back as though he were a longtime friend that he hadn't seen in a while. Mesmerized by the sight of his drug of choice, Kevin didn't know what he was about to be rewarded for, but he was ready to accept it. He stood with his chest puffed out.

With a blunt hanging from his lips, Slick D spoke again. "You came in right on time, my brutha. Today is a celebration! In honor of such a successful month, you can get double the supply." He grinned with confidence.

Remembering the last offer he had accepted from Slick D when he was in one of his good moods and the bloody aftermath he had suffered when Slick D's mood changed back, Kevin declined the offer, shaking his head as he spoke.

"Naw, man. Let me just get a pack tonight."

A pack was one bag of five capsules, and it would set him back seventy-five dollars.

Slick D smiled. "All right, man. I'll get your usual."

Slick D reached over to the pile of bags on the table and grabbed two packs.

"This one's on the house, man. And I'm not taking no for an answer."

Kevin looked at his open hand with apprehension.

"When I say something is on the house, that's exactly what I mean. Now take it," he said with forced assurance.

Kevin extended his hand and, still holding his suspicions, accepted the two packs from Slick D. He pulled out his rolled up wad of cash and counted out seventy-five dollars.

Slick D put his arm around Kevin as he escorted him to the door. Once they got to the door, Kevin stuffed the two small packs into his front pocket.

Slick D shook hands with Kevin, and the man guarding the door opened it.

"All right, man. I'll catch you next time," Slick D offered.

"All right, man."

And with that, Kevin left Slick D's behind and took his time walking to the abandoned house. The accommodations were a far cry from the hotel, and Kevin slightly dreaded being surrounded by junkies. But he had grown accustomed to the environment when it was time for him to ride the wave of his high.

What he was doing was dark. It deserved a dark place, he thought. He picked up his pace as he walked down the street.

The sun was still shining as Kevin neared the flophouse about thirty-five minutes later. He slowly approached the front door, knowing he would be immersed in darkness once he entered. He walked up to the door and turned the latch that he knew was never locked.

As soon as he opened the door, the darkness enveloped him. Some people moved around, but most were motionless, like mannequins propped against walls and lying prone on the floor.

Kevin walked in slow motion toward his usual room, hearing moans before he had reached the doorway. He walked into the dim room and paused to let his eyes adjust. He saw a man lying on the soiled mattress with a woman on top of him, rocking back and forth as he grabbed her hips, guiding her down onto his manhood.

The woman moaned in pleasure and lifted her bottom up and down, controlling the pace, either not noticing Kevin or not caring.

With his eyes glued to the scene before him, Kevin walked over to a broken dresser and pulled one of the packs out of his pocket. He was barely able to see what he was doing, but he could hear.

"Oh yes, baby!" the woman shouted as she reached her climax.

Kevin poured the contents of one capsule onto the wooden dresser, then pulled out the business card that Tanya had given him. He neatly lined up the powdered heroin. He bent down and inhaled deeply.

The couple's pace quickened, and the man began to groan. Before the man could climax, another woman walked in and began to suck on the first woman's nipple. They both looked tantalizing as their silhouettes moved in the darkness. The woman riding moaned.

Kevin stared at the scene as his own manhood hardened.

He pulled out another capsule and poured the contents onto the top of the dresser. He bent down once more and inhaled deeply. Beginning to feel the wave of his high, Kevin stumbled to a spot on the wall as he watched the scene progress.

The woman who had joined the session placed her body on top of the man's face and began to ride. The man's pace slowed as he began to taste the woman who had joined in.

The woman began to moan as her hips began to move back and forth toward her climax. The woman didn't speak; she only moaned in pleasure.

The first woman began to ride the man harder as her second climax was beginning to build.

Kevin, feeling the effects of his high, began to drift off. He passed out into heavenly bliss with images of the erotic scene he had witnessed replaying in his head.

When he finally awoke, he was disoriented. He was sitting on the floor with his back against a wall, and the pockets of his jeans had been turned inside out. He continued to stare at them numbly, then he noticed that he was completely alone in the room. The silence was unusual. His head pounded in his hazy confusion, and reality came back to him.

CHAPTER 9

Saying her goodbyes to Vivian and hugging her before she locked the door, Bianca assured her friend, just as she did every night, that she would be safe walking home. She had attached her mace to her key chain, which she promised to hold in her hand as she walked.

"I look forward to seeing you in the morning." Vivian hugged her tightly one more time.

"See you in the morning, honey." She wiggled her keys with her arms around her friend and employee.

They released each other simultaneously.

As Bianca moved a few steps away, she turned back to see Vivian waving as she entered her car. She waved back and turned to walk to the end of the block.

Someone was standing at the corner, she noted. She gripped her keys tightly in her hand, ready to use her mace if necessary. She recognized his face as soon as he turned around. It was Michael, waiting casually at the corner with his hands in his pockets.

She stopped a few steps before reaching him.

"I thought of a thousand excuses but couldn't come up with something clever enough other than I can't stop thinking about you. Can I walk you to your car?" He was smiling that blush-inducing smile of his.

Now it was her turn to smile as she loosened her grip on her keys and let them dangle from one finger.

"No, because I don't have a car to walk to. I live close enough to walk." She stepped forward as she twirled her keys on her finger, brushing past him and stopping at the corner.

Without hesitation, he extended his hand to her. She instinctively grabbed it, and they walked in silence for a few seconds.

"So how was your day?" he asked casually.

"What are you doing here?"

"Well, you had a full house at lunchtime today, and I missed our usual banter," he chuckled. "I stood at that corner, thinking of every lie possible so that you wouldn't think I was stalking you. Coming up with nothing was a bummer."

"It was a busy house today, but I'm grateful for the business."

"Yeah, it seems your lunch special has become a success."

"And I'm appreciative for it. There were definitely some rough patches along the way. But through everything I have prevailed."

"And that has made you a strong, sexy woman." His voice was sultry this time.

They had made it to the corner of her block, and Bianca hesitated to move forward.

Michael stopped and looked at her with a question in his eyes.

She pulled him to the left. "This way."

Michael walked a few steps behind her, gripping her hand just a little tighter. He released her hand as she walked up to the front door.

Just as she stuck the key in the keyhole, she turned around. "Would you like to come in?"

In that moment, Michael stepped forward, pushing Bianca against her front door. He kissed her deeply. He broke their lips apart. "I thought you'd never ask."

She turned around and unlocked the door. Her heart was pounding as she hung her keys on the hook inside the door and stepped forward.

Michael closed the door behind him and turned the lock. He walked up behind her and began to kiss the back of her neck in the fading evening light.

Bianca let out a moan.

Michael smiled as he continued to kiss her, his hands finding their way under her shirt.

She gasped when his hand found her breast and played with her nipple.

"This is all I have been able to think about for the last week," he whispered in her ear.

She began to feel the growing bulge in his jeans, and it increased her wetness. Her legs weakened as he kissed down her neck to her shoulders. She lifted her hands so that he could remove her shirt from behind. She unsnapped her dark gray slacks then turned around to pull his shirt from his black jeans.

Michael slid his hand inside the front of her boy shorts, and she moaned from the warmth of his touch.

"Wet, just how I like it."

He pulled her pants and boy shorts down with both hands and dropped to his knees. He immediately began to suck her clit.

Bianca grabbed the back of his head in pleasure and moaned. Her legs began to give as her climax neared. Her breath deepened as her legs began to shake.

Michael brought her down to the hardwood floor to finish the job. She screamed in climax as she came all over his face.

Michael surfaced with his face glistening with her juices and unzipped his pants, exposing a rock hard dick that throbbed lightly in anticipation. He inserted himself into the warmth of her essence. Stroking her slowly, he groaned in pleasure.

The coolness of the floor only increased her arousal as she grinded with the flow of his stroke, enjoying every minute and on her way to her second climax. Her body began to tighten and rise up from the floor as she allowed him to go deeper inside her.

At the peak of her climax, Michael pulled out and buried his face in her center as she exploded all over his face for the second time.

He then inserted his still hard manhood again, this time increasing the pace and deepening his stroke.

Bianca cried out instantly in pleasure as his stroke deepened and his manhood got harder.

Delirious with pleasure, Bianca began to scream. "Yes, baby! Make me cum! Make me cum all over this dick!"

Hearing those words only increased Michael's speed, encouraging his own climax. Getting closer to his breaking point, he slowed down, and Bianca came hard and long with a scream of pleasure.

"I am not done with you yet," he murmured.

Michael stood up and offered her his hand. Out of breath, she reluctantly reached for it, and he pulled her to her feet.

She guided him to her bedroom, removed her bra, and lay down on the bed, watching his every move and waiting on him to join her. His eyes stayed locked on hers the entire time.

As soon as he was completely undressed, he climbed on top of her. Grabbing her hair, he kissed her lips first, then her neck, then her shoulders, then each breast, and kissed a trail down to her navel. He stopped just above her pelvis, and she quivered slightly.

He sat up, and his hands began to trail her body.

"Damn, you feel so good." His voice was deep and raspy.

As his hands continued to explore her body, she grabbed his thick hard dick and began to stroke it.

He moaned in pleasure. Moving her hands, he inserted himself inside her with a force that caused them both to inhale. This time his stroke was hard and fast as he took pleasure in her cries of ecstasy.

Her hips rose, signaling that another climax was on its way. She could see the fire in Michael's eyes, the grin on his face as his stroke intensified, daring her climax to reach its peak.

A few strokes later, her legs began to shake as she climaxed hard from his penetration. Her cries sent him over the edge and into his own explosion as he groaned, releasing his semen inside her.

She laid still, unable to move. He found a comfortable space in the bed and put his arm around her. She adjusted so that her head rested on his chest, and they both stared up at the ceiling in silence.

"Well, that was . . . ," her sentence trailed off.

"Yeah," he said, still trying to catch his breath.

CHAPTER 10

The smell of cologne made Bianca's nose wrinkle. She opened her eyes and looked over at a sexy, sleeping, chocolate man who was just beginning to stir in the morning sunlight. When his eyes opened, he smiled.

"Well, this definitely beats waking up alone."

Bianca blushed as she smiled back.

"Let me show you how grateful I am," he added.

Michael turned her on her side away from him and inserted himself inside her immediately. She gripped the side of the bed, bracing herself so that he could go deeper.

"Damn, this shit is so good," he said as he stroked.

He put his hands on top of hers and pushed himself in deeper.

"Cum on this dick one more time for me," he whispered in her ear.

Those words sent her over the edge, and she did as he had asked.

They adjusted their bodies, and Bianca ended up on all fours with Michael behind her.

He buried his face in her sweetness, taking her by surprise, and she began to whimper. He stopped and inserted himself inside her from behind.

He gripped her ass as he went in deeper. Bianca was sure her screams could be heard by her neighbors, but the feeling was just too good to worry about that now.

She gripped the bed and drove her pussy back onto his dick, causing the peak of another climax. She could feel the throbbing anticipation of his climax, and that only caused her to rock harder. Feeling her legs about to give, she came with a shout as he filled her for a second time with his semen.

She fell forward onto the bed and put her hands in her hair, twirling a piece around her finger.

"You're welcome," she said, out of breath.

Michael burst into laughter, trying to catch his own breath and sat back on his legs.

"Did I forget to say thank you?" His tone had curiosity in it.

Her response was a smile that he couldn't see.

He found a space in the bed next to her.

Sucking in a deep breath of air, he put his arm above her head. She adjusted, finding her way onto her back and rested her head on his arm.

They laid there speechless for a moment.

Bianca's growling stomach broke their silence.

Michael burst into laughter. "I guess you worked up an appetite," he joked.

Bianca playfully hit his chest. "*We* worked up an appetite!"

Seconds later, Michael heard his own stomach, and they both burst into laughter in unison.

Searching the room first with her eyes, Bianca made a bee-line for a pink shirt that she spotted on the floor in the corner.

"Breakfast doesn't sound like a bad idea," she said, pulling the shirt over her head.

Michael didn't move. He just nodded his head in agreement with a charming smile.

She nodded her head as well and couldn't help but rest her eyes on his naked body. She felt a blush start to rise in her cheeks and turned and headed for the doorway before he could notice. She heard him getting more comfortable as she walked down the short hall toward the kitchen.

She opened the fridge and grabbed a carton of eggs, shredded cheese, and milk. Then, over to the cabinet, she grabbed pancake mix and set the contents on the counter. Going back to the refrigerator, she opened the freezer and found a box of sausage patties. Satisfied with her choices, she pulled out some pots and pans and started cooking.

After about ten minutes, the aroma of breakfast filled the air. Bianca heard the shower turn on and smiled. He finally decided to get up, she thought.

Bianca let her mind wander. She wasn't quite sure about Michael or if the sex would happen again. But one thing was certain: what Michael had provided her body, she had been craving for weeks.

She bit down on her bottom lip as images of last night and this morning resurfaced in her head. She could admit the sex was good, but she wasn't quite ready to make it a regular event. She thought about Kevin, not knowing when he would reappear.

She was startled back to reality when Michael put his hands around hers as she flipped the sausage patties.

"Damn, you got it smelling good in here," he said, his breath catching her ear and sending a chill down her spine.

"The food will be ready in about fifteen minutes."

With his arms around her, she could feel and see that he was fully clothed.

"I can't let you leave on an empty stomach."

He released her and stepped back, causing her to turn around to face him. For a second, he just stood there, surveying her body, with a smirk on his face.

She crossed her arms in rebellion, her shirt rising slightly, exposing more of her thighs. His eyes moved to the bottom hem of the raised shirt, and Bianca could see the bulge in his pants grow. Her eyes moved to the clock on the wall as the air held a pending question. It was nearing eight, and Bianca was glad she had given Vivian a key to the bakery.

"By the look on your face, breakfast isn't what you have in mind." She danced around the impending question.

"As tempting as that sounds, work is definitely in my near future."

The fire that was in his eyes only moments before had been extinguished. His voice had taken on more of a tone of appreciation rather than lust.

Bianca turned back around and flipped the sausage patties for the last time. Only a few seconds later, she could feel his hand grip her ass and his lips on her neck. She allowed herself to enjoy the simple pleasure of being kissed as her eyes closed.

"Didn't you just say something about work a second ago?" Her voice was barely audible when she spoke, but she knew that he heard every word because his lips formed a smile into her neck and his head lifted.

"I know what I said," he whispered in her ear, then backed away and moved toward the cabinets. He opened one, then another, then another, until he found plates.

He didn't bother to ask where things were in her kitchen; he just searched until he found what he needed.

Her finished breakfast consisted of stacks of pancakes, eggs, and sausage patties, and Michael surveyed the breakfast with hungry eyes.

"If everything tastes as good as it looks, you might have a frequent visitor on your hands. I can't remember the last time I had a home-cooked meal."

They each filled their plates with food and sat down in the dining room.

Bianca picked up her fork, ready to dive into her cheesy eggs, and Michael grabbed her hand and smiled.

Grabbing her other hand, he bowed his head to pray. "Dear Lord, thank you for the nourishment of this food and the hands that prepared it. Amen." His head lifted, and his eyes were on hers as he picked up his fork.

"I can't remember the last time I said grace," she said, picking her fork back up.

"You should make it a habit. I may not be an avid church-goer, but I give thanks when I can," he said with a mouthful of food.

There was little talking while they both enjoyed the delicious breakfast.

When they had both finished, Michael grabbed his plate and rose from the seat. Walking alongside her chair, he picked up her empty plate as well and headed to the kitchen.

Once he made it to the sink, he spoke. "Well, I hate to eat and run, but I do need to head out."

He surveyed the room for his phone, and his eyes landed on it sitting on the living room table. He walked over and grabbed it.

"What's your number? I would hate to have to ambush you every time we met," he chuckled.

She recited her number sarcastically then heard the vibration of her phone ringing.

"Lock me in when you get a chance." He then placed his phone in his back pocket and headed for the door.

As his hand touched the doorknob, Bianca stood up from the chair. He paused, allowing her time to meet him at the door. When he could feel her presence, he turned around to face her.

She stopped in her tracks, almost running into him.

He grabbed both of her arms to steady her and smiled. "Until next time." He bent down and kissed her lips softly. When he lifted his head, he smiled and released her arms. He turned back to the door and grabbed the knob.

Just before making his final exit, he turned to her and said simply, "Have a great day at work."

The door made the sound of its final closure, leaving Bianca standing in solitude, left to her thoughts.

CHAPTER 11

Kevin blinked a few times, waiting for his eyes to adjust to the darkness. With his head pounding, he attempted to rise to his feet. Once he was up, he stumbled backward into the wall.

He looked down at his turned out pockets again, but this time he shoved them back into place. Still foggy, he stumbled over to the dresser and saw that it was clear.

Placing his hands on the dresser, the coolness woke up Kevin just a little bit more, and his memory started to come back to him in pieces.

In an instant, he was digging through his pockets, looking for both his money and the baggies he had gotten from Slick D. When he came up empty-handed, Kevin began to panic. Pacing the floor, he realized he had been robbed.

"Fuck! I should've been more careful!" he scolded himself.

He continued to pace the floor, not sure where to go, not sure how to act. He played out different scenarios for finding the threesome of people who had been in the dark room. But he couldn't conjure up an accurate picture of any of them in his mind. He thought about stealing drugs from another passed out soul in the house. But decided against that. There should, in a perfect world, be honor among thieves and junkies.

He was left with no choice but to do what he did best. Go out into the streets, collect enough money again, and visit Slick D, who no doubt would be entertained by the bullshit that had just happened to him. He would steal enough money to get a hotel room again, where there would be no one to steal from him.

Shaking his head in agreement with himself, Kevin headed for the closed door to exit the house on a mission of recovery.

Once he got out the front door, the summer breeze hit his face invitingly. He walked out to the sidewalk enjoying the night air. He thought of where to go. The park down the street would have easy targets, he thought.

He made a left once he hit the corner about six houses down, changing his direction. The park Kevin was headed to was known for its late night live bands. There would be plenty of people standing or sitting around, enjoying the music or deep in conversation.

Just his type of crowd, Kevin thought. Distracted people—always the easiest targets.

Once Kevin reached the park, he immediately noticed it wasn't as crowded as he had expected.

There were a few amateur singers, dancers, and performers scattered down the long path. A handful of spectators milled about, holding what looked like cups or cans in their hands.

So they have probably been drinking too. This must be my lucky night, Kevin thought as he surveyed the scene. Looking at each person closely, he picked his target: a young woman with a small white crossbody purse with the snap undone. She was holding a cup in her hand, and an amateur R&B singer was serenading her. She was vibing to the song, which Kevin thought he recognized as being from the early 2000s.

Kevin smiled as he approached. The young woman was laughing and joking with a friend standing next to her. Kevin took the opportunity to inch closer to the young woman, all the while maintaining his focus on the singer.

The young woman must have sensed his movements. She turned around and looked right at him. Admiring his attractiveness, she smiled.

"Well, hello there, sexy." When she spoke, her voice was chipper and elevated.

Her friend grabbed her arm. "Mary, stop talking to strangers. Leave that man alone," the petite woman cautioned, peering over Mary's shoulder at Kevin.

Mary leaned into her friend to speak something in her ear. Her open purse was right in front of Kevin, and he moved his hand in quickly, grasping her wallet.

"Hey! What are you doing, man?" a man called from the crowd.

Everyone turned their attention toward the man and then quickly followed his glare in the direction of Kevin, whose hand was frozen under the flap of Mary's purse.

Both women's faces went from shock to anger in a matter of seconds.

Kevin withdrew his hand swiftly and started running.

"Hey, wait!" both women cried in unison.

No one followed Kevin. He ran, and everyone else stood in shock. Even the singer was silenced.

Kevin bolted behind a line of trees then cut across the block to reach a street on the outskirts of the park. He crossed the street without breaking stride, fortunate that there was no traffic, and cut between the first two tall buildings that he came across and paused to catch his breath.

He looked down at his hands and realized they were empty. Aggravated with himself for his carelessness, he began to pace the space between the two buildings.

This was the first time he had been unsuccessful in getting what he wanted. Kevin was shocked but also furious. He was able to be so cunning before. How had he let himself get caught? Had he become overconfident and cocky?

On his fourth trip up and down the alley between the buildings, Kevin heard the distinct sound of a car unlocking, and in a rage, he headed toward the sound.

He quickly searched the ground near a pair of dumpsters for something to use as a weapon and found a narrow wooden plank. Grabbing it, he pressed forward, willing to do what it took this time to collect the re-up he needed.

When he got to the opening where the alley met the sidewalk, he glanced left and saw a man standing by a shiny black car with his head down, about to get inside.

Kevin immediately rushed the man, raising the plank and striking the back of the man's legs. He crumpled to the ground, more surprised than injured.

"Give me your muthafuckin wallet!" Kevin shouted.

The man fumbled first in his front pocket as he groaned from the shock and reached his arm behind him and into his back pocket.

"Don't fuckin look at me!" Kevin screamed, snatching the wallet from the man's hand.

The man bowed his head, and Kevin took off, running until he couldn't take another step. He stopped at Main and South Harwood to catch his breath. Above him, the sign read Hotel Indigo Dallas Downtown.

He opened the man's wallet that he gripped tightly in his hand. But before he could count any money, a beautiful woman came out of the hotel doors and lit a cigarette. She noticed him immediately and began to walk in his direction.

"Well, hello there, stranger. You not from around here?" The woman had a southern accent.

Closing the wallet, Kevin faced the woman. "No, I'm not. Why do you ask?"

"I got a room upstairs if you're looking for a warm place to lay your head." She grinned as she puffed on her cigarette.

Kevin considered his options, weighing the pros and cons of sex with this unknown woman. He decided to take his chances.

"What brings you out so late at night?" she asked, continuing her attempt at light conversation.

"The night is when I come alive," he said with seduction.

"Well, I'm looking forward to making it more interesting." She put her hand on his chest.

"Why don't we head upstairs?" Kevin suggested, grabbing her hand from his chest.

She threw down her half-smoked cigarette and snuffed it out with a red stiletto. Together they turned and went inside the hotel. Kevin was taken aback by what he saw. From the outside, the hotel's façade was beige and plain, but inside, the décor was breathtaking and contemporary. The floors were covered in white marble, and the countertops at the front desk were white to match. The sofas in the lobby offered a stark contrast in solid black leather. A crystal chandelier sparkled above a coffee table.

"My name is Maria, by the way," she offered once they reached the silver elevator doors. She turned and smiled at him, entering the elevator doors as soon as they opened. He followed her inside and watched her press button number six.

They rode the elevator in silence, each in their own thoughts.

Once the doors opened, Maria stepped out first and turned left. Kevin followed behind her. She stopped at the hotel room that was numbered in gold letters, 618, and used her key card to enter the room. The room's décor mirrored the lobby's, with white marble flooring and a queen-sized bed draped with a black comforter and accented with gray pillows.

"Why don't you make yourself more comfortable, and I'll be out in just a second." She gestured toward the bed before she entered the bathroom.

Kevin came farther into the room, passed the bathroom door, and sat on the bed. He pulled the stolen wallet from his back pocket and opened it, eager to count the money. He found the man's ID, a few credit cards, and a picture of a dog. There was no cash at all. Kevin was furious.

"Fuck!" he shouted. He stood up from the bed with the open wallet in his hand and began pacing the floor in anger.

He heard Maria shout from the bathroom, "Is everything all right out there?"

She emerged from the bathroom wearing nothing but a lace panty and bra set. She eyed the open empty wallet in his hand, and her face went from confusion to anger.

"I hope you weren't under the impression that this pussy was free because it's not!"

Already filled with rage, Kevin turned in her direction ready to pounce.

"Listen, you little bitch! I don't pay for pussy!" He stormed up to her and slapped her hard in the face.

She grabbed her face and ran to a table, picking up a hunting knife that Kevin hadn't noticed. She lunged at him, attempting to stab him but missed.

In his attempt to evade the knife, Kevin tripped over a chair leg and they both fell to the floor.

She was strong and adrenaline-fueled, but Kevin managed to gain control of the knife. Their struggle continued, each of them getting nicked by the knife as their arms grappled wildly to inflict any damage possible.

Both were wide-eyed and getting sweaty, drawing upon all the strength they had to simply stay alive. A sickening squish sound—like the sound of a tire being punctured—interrupted the sounds of their frantic gasps for air, and a blood stain began to spread across Kevin's shirt.

He watched as the life began to drain out of Maria's eyes and pushed her off of him as her breath became shallow. Her body fell limply to the floor beside him. She tried to take a breath—to speak—but the remaining light in her eyes dimmed completely.

Kevin sat up and rested his back against the end of the bed. He looked down at hands that were covered in blood. Then he looked down at his blood-covered shirt and started to panic.

Rising to his feet, he screamed at the woman lying dead on the floor. "Look what you made me do!"

He looked at himself in the room's full-length mirror and shuddered at his reflection. His shirt and hands were covered in blood. His skin was clammy. The metallic odor of Maria's blood was mingling with the stench of his own sweat.

He'd have to find a side stairwell. He couldn't walk back through the main entrance—too many people. But first, he had to do something about the blood on his hands. He stepped into the hotel bathroom and washed his hands and face. That was the best he was going to be able to do. He grabbed an extra towel from the bar over the toilet.

He paused outside of the bathroom and looked at the woman lying lifeless on the floor. He approached her, careful not to step in any blood, and bent down to wipe off the handle of the knife, which was still stuck in her abdomen.

He had to get the hell out of there. Seconds counted. What if someone showed up at her door? What if someone had heard their scuffle? There was only one place he knew he could go under any circumstances. Making his mind up, he turned the doorknob with the white towel and was relieved to see an empty hallway. He made a left toward a marked stairwell and jogged down six flights of stairs to a side door that opened onto a sidewalk.

He welcomed the cool breeze that hit his face, but he had a big problem. He couldn't walk around in a blood-soaked shirt. Keeping in the shadows as much as possible, he scanned the nearby parking lots for a clothing donation bin. He spotted one just a block away across the street and knew that was his best bet. He made his way quickly, with his head down and his hands in the front pockets of his jeans, hoping that his arms would partially obscure the blood stains.

Once he reached the bin, he stuck his hand inside and tried his luck. On the first attempt, he pulled out a woman's blouse. Throwing it back inside, he tried again and came up with a tattered black leather jacket suitable for a man or a woman.

He yanked the jacket on over his shirt to see how much it covered. The sleeves were short on him, but it would have to do.

Kevin walked quickly with only one destination in mind.

CHAPTER 12

Today had been a perfect day, Bianca thought as she looked around at the few people still lingering in her small dining area. The crowd had been medium-sized for most of the day, but her favorite part had been when Michael came in for lunch.

She had thoroughly enjoyed serving her customers while casually flirting with Michael. And he had willingly taken part in the banter. It seemed as if the day had flown by, and when the last of the lunch crew had made their exit, Michael had approached the counter.

"You look beautiful today." His voice was deep and low, forcing her to look up from the counter she had been wiping down.

She had worn a dark purple V-neck shirt and a black and white pin-striped skirt that came to her ankles.

"Thank you," she had blushed.

He had grabbed her hand and repeated his words.

"You look beautiful today." This time his tone had taken on a different meaning.

Not only had Bianca blushed, but she had also felt a surge of moistness between her legs and had almost made a sound. She slid her hand from underneath his before she spoke.

"Don't you have work to get to?" she had asked him.

Michael had looked down at his watch in response. "It's definitely time for me to go back in. Maybe I'll see you later." He had grabbed her hand and kissed it before leaving the counter and exiting the bakery.

As soon as the glass door had closed behind him, Vivian approached Bianca, wearing a big grin.

"So something has definitely happened between you two. Now spill it!" Vivian had said with one hand on her hip, still wearing a knowing smirk.

"Later," Bianca had mouthed, looking at the remaining customers.

After the last customer had gone, Bianca could wait no longer to hold the secret that had been in the back of her mind all day. With her last reminiscent thoughts still fresh on her mind, she got Vivian's attention. "Our day has been so busy, but I have been dying to fill you in."

"Good, because I feel like this story is going to be cause for a drink!" Vivian walked around the counter to the employee side, reached inside a cabinet and pulled out a bottle of pinot grigio.

Bianca grabbed two plastic cups and put them on the counter in front of them, waiting for her best friend and assistant to pour.

Vivian filled both cups, and both women took a sip of wine before Bianca began. She shared the details of the previous night, beginning with Michael waiting for her on the corner and ending with him leaving this morning after breakfast. Vivian hung on every word, her eyes wide, taking occasional sips of her wine.

"Well, I'll be damned! I hate to say I told you so, but I told you so!" Vivian beamed.

Bianca laughed and grabbed her own cup from the counter, taking a huge swig before she jumped right back in and added a few more details that she recalled. When she was finished, they both took a drink and laughed.

"Well, damn! Look at you, girl. This was your first time with someone other than Kevin, right?"

"Yeah," Bianca admitted. "And the fucked up thing is, I can see it happening repeatedly in the future!"

The women slapped hands and laughed again.

"But seriously," Bianca broke in. "I love Kevin too much to make the situation with Michael anything more than sex. Sex that could inspire nations, but sex nonetheless."

Vivian looked at her with questioning eyes. "If you say so, hon. Finish what you're doing so that we can lock up. I would never let you close the bakery alone."

"Almost done," Bianca said, gathering up the last of the dishes. She stacked everything in the sink and rinsed them with some hot water.

"I'll come in early tomorrow and load everything into the dishwasher. I am just as ready to go as you are tonight." Bianca turned off the water and dried her hands on a towel. Grabbing the shop keys and her purse, Bianca headed for the door with Vivian following close behind.

Once Bianca had locked up, Vivian hugged her hard.

"OK, girl, you know that I love you. I will see you in the morning. Don't get into any trouble tonight," Vivian teased, giving Bianca a playful pat on her bottom.

"Yes, mother. I will behave myself tonight." Bianca rolled her eyes.

"Don't you roll your eyes at me!" Vivian said, playing along.

"You think you know everything."

"No, I just know *you*."

They released each other's embrace.

"Bye, love," Bianca said as she turned to walk away.

Vivian waited until Bianca made it to the corner, just like every night.

Once she got to the corner, Bianca turned around to see Vivian heading toward her car.

Bianca continued her walk to her front door, anxious to have some solitude. She walked inside, locked the door behind her, and went straight to her room to undress.

Following her usual ritual, she stripped down and turned on the shower before heading back to the kitchen to pour a healthy glass of chardonnay. She inhaled deeply. She was no wine expert, but she knew she liked her chardonnay extra dry and oaky. She returned to her bedroom and set her wine on the nightstand before walking back into the bathroom. The hot shower water had already started to steam up the bathroom mirrors. She looked at the distorted image of herself and smiled.

She stepped into the shower and slowly bathed herself, enjoying the scent of the vanilla body wash and the feel of the hot water on her skin. As she rinsed the last of the soap off her body, she reluctantly turned off the water and pulled back the shower curtain. Not worrying about a towel or robe, she entered her bedroom and headed straight for the wine glass, which had begun to sweat.

She took a large gulp and sighed. Business was so good, but that also meant that she came home exhausted almost every evening.

With the glass still in her hand, Bianca sat down on top of her perfectly made bed. Putting the glass down, she burrowed under the covers, letting the sheets dry the remaining wetness on her body. Time for another gulp, she thought, and took one before easing down lower in the bed, giving in to an early bedtime. She was completely relaxed and comfortable, and had no trouble drifting off.

In her dream, she was walking in a field of tall grass speckled with wildflowers in a rainbow of colors. The sun was shining brightly in a cloudless sky, and Bianca could feel the warmth on her skin.

She walked through the field barefoot and came to a road. From each direction of the road, she could hear a man calling her name. She recognized both voices. From her left, it was definitely Michael's voice, and to her right, it was Kevin's.

She turned and headed in the direction of the person she loved the most.

Once she reached Kevin, she was thankful for what she saw before her eyes. Kevin looked like his old self. He was clean-shaven, wearing a neatly pressed white dress shirt and medium-dark jeans that faded in color down the front.

He smiled as she approached, and Bianca fell in love all over again. They hugged as soon as she was near enough to touch him.

They released each other, and Bianca stood silent, waiting for Kevin to speak.

"Thank you for waiting for me," he said softly. "I've never met another person who has loved me so much."

When Bianca opened her mouth to respond, no sound came out. She looked at him, puzzled, but he just smiled.

"It's OK. You don't have to say anything. I can show you how I feel better than I can tell you."

Kevin stepped forward and swept her into his arms, kissing her deeply. As their kisses became more feverish, Kevin loosened the tie on the white wrap dress that Bianca didn't realize she was wearing. She let out a low moan in anticipation.

He stopped, breaking their embrace. He took her hand and walked her to a clearing in the field where a checkered fleece blanket had appeared seemingly out of nowhere.

Bianca reclined on the blanket, and Kevin parted her legs. Without hesitation, he began to work his tongue over her clit. She moaned in pleasure, grabbing the grass alongside the blanket. She could feel her climax nearing, forcing her back to arch.

Kevin quickened his pace, welcoming her climax, and Bianca came with a loud cry.

Kevin sat up, the lower half of his face shining from her juices, and undid his belt, unzipped his jeans, and allowed his rock hard manhood to burst from his boxer shorts. He inserted himself inside of her with full force and a sense of urgency as he went deep inside her.

She expected his rhythm to be fast, but instead, it was slow and steady. Every stroke intentional. They moaned together, each of them finding pleasure in every sensation.

She could feel her second climax building, and so could he.

He increased his speed, causing her breath to increase in speed. He laid his body on top of hers and lifted her legs, going deeper inside of her.

She was near the edge, and she could tell that he was too. Each stroke was pure ecstasy. She had missed this—and him—so much.

Then . . . Bianca heard a knock.

At first she ignored it, savoring the building anticipation of the climax. But the knock came again, persistent and louder.

She awoke disoriented.

The first thing that came into focus was her bedroom ceiling. She had left a light on in the bathroom. Then three hard knocks came again, forcing Bianca to sit up. Glancing down at her naked body, she grabbed her robe from the hook behind the bathroom door.

What time was it? she wondered. Her evening came back to her. She had showered and had some wine before collapsing. She tied her robe and made her way to the front door. In a moment of clarity, she recalled Michael hinting at the possibility that he would drop by. She smiled at the thought and looked through the peephole.

No one was there. The knock came again. But it was behind her. At that moment, she knew without question who was at the door.

She could see the familiar silhouette standing at her patio door. She opened it, and what she saw horrified her.

Kevin stood before her, the lower half of his shirt covered in something dark. He looked more disheveled than usual, and his eyes were wild. He wore a leather jacket that was far too small for him and the same dark gray shirt and jeans that she had given him the last time he was there.

"I fucked up, B."

He hadn't called her B since the second year of their marriage. Mindlessly, without looking away from eyes that revealed a mixture of terror and desperation, she unlocked the screen door and let him in.

He paced frantically, with his hands gripping the sides of his head.

"I don't know what happened," he blurted out. "The bitch pulled a knife on me! And now she's dead," he added, after steeling himself for a moment. He seemed to be talking as much to himself as he was to Bianca.

"Who's dead? What happened?" Bianca stepped closer to him when she spoke and switched on the kitchen light. It took a few seconds for her eyes to adjust, and then she saw it: more than half of Kevin's shirt was covered in what looked like dried blood.

Doing her best to stay calm, she walked up to him, stopped him from pacing, and spoke, looking him in the eyes. "Tell me what's going on." There was sincere concern in her voice.

Kevin immediately broke down. There was no sense hiding anything from Bianca anymore. This was rock bottom. And any chance he had of climbing his way out would have to involve her. He told her everything that had happened that night, from getting caught in the park trying to take the young woman's wallet, to attacking the man on the street for his, and ending up in Maria's hotel room where his will to survive had clouded his thinking and he had killed her. By the time Kevin finished his story, he was on his knees in front of Bianca, his arms around her legs.

"Please help me." There was genuine sadness in his voice.

Bianca was familiar with this tone. It was the same one he had used when he had gotten beaten up months before. She rubbed his head in an attempt to console him.

Kevin had finally realized the severity of his addiction and began to sob into her bare legs.

She stood still, allowing him to release his emotions for a few minutes. Then she pointed his head up in her direction. "Did anyone see you?"

"I made sure they didn't."

Helping him to his feet, she took his hand and led him to her master bathroom. He sat on the closed lid of the toilet seat as she undressed him down to his boxers.

She pulled the shower curtain back and turned on the water, adjusting the temperature to a comfortable level. She walked back over to him and gestured for him to stand.

He rose and pulled off his boxers with what little strength he had left. He stepped into the shower, and Bianca collected his clothes from the floor.

"What are you doing with my clothes?" he said, almost at a whisper.

"I don't know, but I'll think of something."

She went to her kitchen and got a trash bag from under the kitchen sink and stuffed his clothes inside. Dropping the bag on the kitchen floor, she headed back to the bedroom. She sat on the end of the bed, still wearing nothing but her robe. Fragments of her dream popped in and out of her head, and she heard him turn off the shower water.

She stood up and grabbed a bath towel that was sitting on top of her dirty clothes basket, and as soon as he stepped out of the shower, she began to dry his body.

He stopped her, grabbing both of her hands.

She looked up at him with a question in her eyes.

Without saying a word, he bent down and kissed her passionately.

Her legs began to weaken, and she let out a moan and dropped the towel that was barely in her hands.

Once the towel hit the floor, Kevin pushed her against the counter until she was sitting on it. With her legs open, he moved in between them, kissing her neck, shoulders, and back to her lips.

She moaned in pleasure, feeling her horniness rise and her wetness increase as his manhood rubbed against her clit. Just like in her dream, he entered her without hesitation, triggering a few seconds of déjà vu. She moaned and grabbed his back as he stroked her slowly and deeply, making every stroke intentional as he kissed and sucked her neck.

She wrapped her legs around him and squeezed, allowing him to go deeper. She could feel her climax building the more he stroked. When she came, it was hard and breathless.

Kevin stepped back and put his hand out to help her off the counter and guided her to the bed. When they reached it, he guided her down and began to devour her. She could not hold back her cries of pleasure as he worked his tongue around her clit, then dipped his tongue in and out of her wet and dripping center.

She grabbed his head, whispering his name. "Oh yes, Kevin." Her voice cracked as he moved back to her clit and began to suck and lick the head. Her hips began to rock on his face as her climax was reaching its peak. She let out a loud scream as she exploded all over his face. Her chest heaved as she attempted to catch her breath.

He stopped briefly then began licking her clit again, taking pleasure in sending her into a state of total delirium.

Then he inserted his tongue inside the river that was beginning to flow from her, suddenly going a little lower to lick the finishing drops of her orgasm that moistened her asshole. His tongue swirled around her asshole and was inserted, and she came again.

Satisfied with his performance, he inserted himself inside her, stroking at a quicker pace as he enjoyed the wetness, not quite ready for his own climax. He stopped for a few seconds and flipped her over on all fours. He inserted himself from behind and slapped her ass as he pumped in and out. Feeling her muscles begin to contract, signaling another climax, Kevin decided that this was the perfect time for him to climax as well.

His pace quickened as he could feel his own climax approaching. By this time, Bianca was screaming in ecstasy with every stroke. Spreading her ass cheeks apart to go just a little bit deeper, Kevin could feel her release as he released with a deep groan, coming hard inside her.

Out of breath, he fell to the bed next to her as her body straightened. He kissed the back of her shoulder as she laid there silent, unable to move, and he had his own déjà vu moment and smiled.

Within minutes, they were both fast asleep. Kevin's arms were wrapped around Bianca as they cuddled peacefully and rested comfortably in a way that neither of them had in months.

Bianca awoke about three hours later, still wrapped in arms that held her tightly, as if a life depended on it. She eased out of his embrace on a mission, not wanting to disturb him. He just moved over to his dedicated side of the bed without opening his eyes. Bianca waited a few minutes to make sure he was still asleep before slowly getting up from the bed.

She went to her dirty clothes basket, grabbed a pair of dark denim jeans and an oversized black t-shirt that she had slept in the week before. She left the bedroom, quietly closing the door behind her.

CHAPTER 13

Bianca turned on the kitchen light, went to one of her cabinets, and pulled out some old lighter fluid for the barbecue grill that hadn't been touched since she'd kicked Kevin out. She poured a healthy amount into the trash bag containing Kevin's soiled clothes, making sure all of his clothes were drenched in the fluid. She grabbed a lighter from her kitchen junk drawer and walked out onto her back patio.

A warm breeze greeted her. She hadn't even realized that she was sweating until the wind hit her face. She looked out at her small yard and walked all the way to the back fence where she'd once fantasized about creating a small flower garden. Over time she had collected an assortment of retaining blocks, bricks, and stepping-stones to use in the garden, and she arranged them now in a circle and dropped the bag in the center. She pulled a piece of paper from the trash bin that was outside and lit it, then stuffed it inside the bag and jumped back.

The contents of the trash bag burst into flames that were hot enough to melt the plastic bag. Bianca watched until everything had virtually disintegrated and the fire was almost out.

She went back into the house and grabbed a mop bucket from the pantry. Filling it with water, she brought it back outside and poured it over the dying flame to extinguish it completely. Bianca inspected what was left in the center of the blocks, making sure that every bit of clothing had burned entirely. Only a few pieces of black plastic remained.

She picked up the fragments of the trash bag, placed the blocks and bricks back along the fence, and grabbed the bucket. She looked around to see if any of her neighbors had been stirred by the burning smell and flames. She was relieved to see that no lights on either side of her duplex had been turned on.

The odor of burning plastic hung in the air, and she hoped it would be gone by morning. She stopped at the trash can to throw away the plastic remnants and went inside.

She put the lighter and bucket away and headed back to the bedroom. The clock on her nightstand informed her that it was five thirty. She quickly undressed and got back into bed with Kevin, ready for more sleep.

He stirred slightly when she reentered the bed. She put her arm around him this time and drifted off to sleep.

When they both finally started to stir, Bianca saw daylight streaming through the bedroom blinds. She rolled over to look at the clock. It was a quarter past noon.

She stretched as Kevin woke up completely and turned to face her with a smile.

"What?" She looked at him in the middle of her second stretch.

"I love you. So what are we going to do about my clothes?" His face was serious.

"I burned them in the middle of the night."

They laid together in silence for a few moments, then he leaned in and kissed her before climbing out of bed.

She watched every move of his naked body as he walked over to the set of drawers that had belonged to him and pulled out some boxers. Putting them on, he exited the bedroom.

Bianca laid in the bed a few minutes longer, not wanting to leave the warm, soft comfort.

After a few more minutes, the aroma of sausage filled the air, forcing her out of the bed. Bianca had just realized she was hungry. She threw on an oversized shirt, grabbed the wine glass from her nightstand, and headed to the kitchen.

She watched Kevin as he flipped the sausage patties on the stove.

"I'm not as good a cook as you, but breakfast sandwiches are in the making." Kevin spoke as if he felt proud of himself.

Bianca went to the television in the living room and flipped through the channels in search of a news station. She held her breath, hoping there wouldn't be a report of what had happened the night before. The weatherman was talking about the forecast for the coming week. Bianca exhaled and went back to the kitchen, leaving the news on.

Kevin started talking as he cooked. He told her that he was finally ready to admit to his addiction and seek help for something that he thought he had control over. He talked about how he was ready to get back to being himself. He fantasized about job searches once he was clean, contacts he could call, and interviews he planned to go on.

Bianca listened as she had another moment of déjà vu, reflecting back on the flashes of her dream. She was about to add to the conversation when a breaking news story caught their attention.

"A woman has been found murdered at the Indigo Dallas Hotel. Reports say the woman was fatally stabbed in the abdomen. By the time the paramedics arrived, they found the woman dead on the scene." The female news anchor continued: "Police say there are no suspects yet and that it's early in the investigation. They are looking for anyone who heard or saw anything that could be relevant to the case. The woman has also not been identified."

A local number flashed at the bottom of the screen.

"If anyone knows anything, please use the contact number below. We have someone on location waiting to give us an update later in the broadcast, so stay tuned."

Bianca turned away from the flat screen TV and looked at Kevin.

"Are you sure no one saw you?" Her voice was heavy with emotion when she spoke.

"I'm positive," he said with certainty, moving on to making the eggs for his breakfast sandwiches.

"We can't really be sure of anything right now. I think we should look up a rehabilitation center outside of the city, just in case anything does come up."

"I'm willing to do anything at this point," he agreed.

Bianca got her laptop off the small table in the living room and popped it open on the dining room table.

Kevin finished making their breakfast sandwiches and joined Bianca at the table, placing their plates down and sitting beside her in full view of the monitor.

They ate and searched, pausing to discuss the facilities that caught their eyes. They finished their breakfast but hadn't been able to make a decision.

Kevin cleared their plates and placed them in the sink.

"I'll go wherever you think is best, but it seems like you want me to go too far away."

"It isn't that I want you to be far away from me. I want you far away from everything so that you can recover. We tried a place within the city the first time, and that wasn't good for us at all. I am asking you to give something farther away a chance, and the one I found is covered by our insurance so it won't break the bank," she pleaded.

Seeing the anguish and heartache in her face, he had no choice.

"OK. I'll try."

A low buzz caught their attention, and Bianca walked over to her purse and pulled out her cell phone. Vivian's name flashed across the screen.

Bianca answered just before her voicemail came on.

"Hey, love, did you ditch work today and forget to tell me? It's not like you to not come in. I guess someone did make their appearance last night. I haven't seen him today either. Good for you! You deserve a day off, Ms. B. I'm keeping things in order pretty successfully, but Mr. Reynolds came by with some papers for you to sign. I will just leave them in the back office."

"I definitely have a visitor, but it's not the one you're thinking," she said in a muffled voice before speaking louder. "Kevin says hello."

She mouthed to him that Vivian was on the other end of the line. He nodded and retreated to the bedroom.

"Tell Kevin I said hello," Vivian said dramatically.

Bianca rolled her eyes.

"He's no longer in the room, but I'll tell him in a minute. Now about this paperwork Mr. Reynolds wants me to sign, I'll come in within the next hour and take care of it."

"OK, love. Well, I'm here when you decide to make your entrance. After you finish that up, I want every detail of what's been going on there." Vivian laughed as if she had told a joke.

"You can't even imagine," Bianca said, her tone confirming that there was definitely drama to share. "I'm about to pull myself together. I'll see you in an hour."

"OK, hon. See you when you make it!" Vivian said with enthusiasm, ready to hear the untold secrets of the last twelve hours.

The call ended, and Bianca headed to the bedroom.

When she reached the doorway, she found Kevin relaxing comfortably in the bed. "Will you be fine if I run over to the bakery to sign some paperwork and see how Vivian is doing? I shouldn't be gone long."

His response was casual and unbothered. "I'll be waiting here when you return."

And with that, Bianca went to her closet and grabbed a two-toned black and pink maxi dress, black boy shorts and a bra, and started getting dressed.

Kevin watched her admiringly.

"OK, love. I'll be back in a few hours, and we can discuss our final decision on the rehab center." She leaned over him on the bed and kissed him before retreating from the master bedroom.

Kevin nodded in agreement and turned on the bedroom TV, which hadn't been used since his departure, and began flipping through the channels.

Bianca picked up her purse from the end table near the front door, grabbed her keys, and left the duplex, locking the door behind her.

CHAPTER 14

Bianca spent three hours at the bakery, reading through the new paperwork, helping Vivian with customers, and giving Vivian an edited version of what had happened the night before. It wasn't safe for anyone else to know about Maria or Bianca's little bonfire in the middle of the night. She finished her story on a high note about Kevin's decision to take his recovery seriously and enter rehab.

Vivian was genuinely elated that things had finally turned around for her favorite couple. She'd always said that Bianca and Kevin were meant for one another. She praised Bianca for her sheer will and determination to persevere through such difficult circumstances.

And Vivian doesn't even know the worst of it, Bianca had thought to herself. By the time Bianca had taken the walk home, the sun had started to set.

Filled with renewed enthusiasm for their lives ahead, Bianca unlocked the front door and entered her duplex, already talking.

"Sorry it took me so long, love. There were a lot of small fires to put out at the bakery today. But all has been settled, and we can get back to making a decision."

But no one was there to hear her. The duplex was completely silent. Bianca put her things down and headed straight for the bedroom. No one was there.

She flipped on the light in the bathroom. There was no one there either. She circled every room in a tiny state of confusion.

She stopped in her tracks when she saw that her laptop was no longer on the table in the dining room. She rushed back to the bedroom and flipped on the bedroom light. The flat screen TV from the bedroom was missing, too, and the drawers of Kevin's dresser had all been rummaged through.

"Well, I'll be damned," Bianca uttered in shock.

Kevin had pulled his usual bullshit again. She felt completely devastated.

She went to the kitchen and poured herself the last of the chardonnay that was in there. She took a large gulp and stood there, ready to murder, damage, or hurt anything in sight. She took another gulp and felt her temples pulsate. After everything that had happened, Kevin had run off again with no warning, and she had no idea if or when he would return. And at this point, she wasn't sure she wanted him to.

Once her glass was empty, she filled it a second time with a newly opened bottle. After the second glass of wine was gone, she went back to the refrigerator and poured another.

Maybe he just went out to tie up some loose ends and will be back before the morning, she lied to calm herself.

Feeling the effects of the wine and exhausted from the range of emotions she felt, she began to doze off, falling asleep on the couch, still hoping for a knock at the patio door.

CHAPTER 15

After selling the items he had stolen from Bianca, Kevin was basking in the glow of having money for his next fix when the unthinkable happened.

Kevin got what he needed from Slick D, who was all too happy to supply him with what he had lost two nights ago, and returned to the only place that really felt like home.

Kevin opened up a capsule in the abandoned house and sniffed a line of heroin. He was alone in the bedroom this time; no threesome was taking place on the moldy mattress. He almost felt guilty for what he had done to Bianca, but then he thought about the hell he had gone through and the long journey toward recovery that was expected of him and sniffed a second line from the same capsule.

But the guilt hung on. He took out another capsule, broke it open, and sniffed another line. The effects were swift, and he never wanted the feeling to dissipate—ever—so he sniffed another line.

The room began to spin. Kevin felt euphoric. He pulled out a third capsule and broke it open, separating the contents into halves as he had the others, and sniffed both lines. He smiled in his highness, not feeling anything at all now.

He found his way to a wall in the dark room and slid down it like he had done so many times before. Only this time, as he floated higher and higher on a cloud of heroin, his mouth began to foam. His legs began to twitch uncontrollably before his body began convulsing violently. He lost control of his bowels.

There was no one there to notice him. There was no one to watch the lights go out in his eyes. He became as lifeless as the hardwood floor itself. As lifeless as the abandoned house.

ABOUT THE AUTHOR

Tina Tennyson was born and raised in Detroit, Michigan. After high school, life took her to Dallas, Texas. In 2011, she obtained her bachelor's degree in early childhood education and married her husband at the age of twenty-five. Her love for writing started young and flourished over the years. She began writing poetry, songs, and a few unpublished short stories. After working in customer service at Neiman Marcus for six years, Tina (also known as ShanTina) decided to take the first step toward becoming an author at the age of thirty-one. This decision came after years of hesitation, but she finally took a leap of faith to make one of her biggest dreams come true. Her main goal as a writer is to make readers feel an emotional connection of empowerment. She released her first novel, Justice Finds Her Way Home, in 2018. Her style of writing is captivating and will leave you wanting more. Prepare yourself to become completely submerged in the journey.

www.ingramcontent.com/pod-product-compliance
Lightning Source LLC
Chambersburg PA
CBHW071130250626
47159CB00006B/2192